MEMORIES ARE THE STORIES WE TELL OURSELVES

Christian Pascale

Lavender Press
An imprint of Blue Fortune Enterprises, LLC

For information contact :
Blue Fortune Enterprises, LLC
Lavender Press
P.O. Box 554
Yorktown, VA 23690
http://blue-fortune.com

Book and Cover design by Raphael Pascale,
deviantart.com/angelusdes1dn, angelxangelus@gmail.com

ISBN: 978-1-948979-38-2
First Edition: August 2020

Dedication

To my wife and kids

ACKNOWLEDGEMENTS

When I was very young, I was an avid reader and, in looking back, I have always wanted to be a writer. I spent time in Paris writing poetry and some prose, but later my work domestically and overseas combined with raising a wonderful family took priority, and I put my desire on the back burner.

Almost three years ago, I gathered my courage and searched the internet for groups of local writers to help me through the often solitary process of writing for publication. I found the Williamsburg Writers to whom I owe a profound debt of gratitude. Participating in this group has enabled me to hone my writing skills. The members encouraged me to find stories I had written over the years and write new ones inspired by my experiences at home and abroad. Any success this book may have is due to the advice and critiques given by members of this group. Not only were their discussions of style invaluable, they helped me clarify the themes that run through all of my stories.

I would like to single out Peter Stipe, Cindy Freeman, Elizabeth Compton Lee, Sharon Dillon, Patti Procopi,

Susan Williamson, and Dave Pistorese for their mentorship. Each writer, in their individual way has contributed to the stories in this book making them stronger, better, and more readable. It is because of them that I have the confidence to believe in what I have written.

I would also like to thank my two sons, Michel for his love and support and Raphael for his continuous artistic and thematic critique. My wife Liria has read my stories and helped me throughout with many realistic details. She calmed my fears, supported me when I became discouraged, and allowed me the necessary times of solitude I needed to write this book.

I deeply appreciate the help of my editor and publisher, Narielle Living. Without her patience, advice, and willingness to take on an unpublished author, this book would never have come to fruition.

Finally, I would like to thank other writers who have reviewed this book and offered their valuable suggestions. If I have forgotten anyone, I hope they will forgive me.

TABLE OF CONTENTS

PREFACE

THIS COLLECTION OF STORIES PRESENTS a mixture of truth and fiction akin to J.D. Salinger's novel Catcher in the Rye" or John Glassco's "Memoirs of Montparnasse."

Sometimes told in the third person and sometimes in first person, the stories have several common themes that reverberate through them. The first series of stories include the themes of innocence, coming of age, finding oneself, being a loner, learning not to judge others, the need for companionship, how to face death, the afterlife, disillusionment with religion, and can we make a difference in this world.

The second series follows a young man's experiences in France. They explore the expat life of a youth who goes in search of adventure and self-knowledge and describe his quest to find himself. In them, he falls in love with a city, deals with jealousy and unrequited love, survives and thrives as a tennis coach, and finally learns, while working at a Club Med, a truth that takes him back to the original memories. These stories capture a rediscovery of what is real, what is valuable and the juxtaposition of internal vs external beauty.

In the last section, four stories, all told in the third person, explore the life of diplomats living in imaginary countries. The stories address social issues such as corruption and violence and the main characters must come to terms with the paradox of encountering wonderful people living in corrupt and violent societies.

I believe that writing is a way of communication with the wider world and a means to transmit something of what we have experienced. Each new experience contributes to who we are, and I would not be who I am without having lived and loved and met such a wide variety of characters. Although some of the stories are not completely true-to-life's experiences, they are based on what I have seen, a reality sometimes ugly, but often wonderful and beautiful. Each experience taught me something of life's basic values. Without the ability to cherish what is good in ourselves and others we have nothing. So I write because I cannot afford not to write, just as I cannot afford not to breath. When I write, I drawn on what is within my soul, an essence which pours out and hopefully allows me to touch the soul of the reader. Happy reading.

1
THE DANCE

JOANNE WAS MY SOUL MATE. We first met in third grade at Berkeley Academy, and she had sparkling cornflower-blue eyes and a smile that made me light-headed. Her shoulder-length hair shimmered like sunlight over water. Unfortunately for me, boys were required to leave the school after sixth grade, and once I obtained a scholarship to an all-boys preparatory school, I rarely saw Joanne. We met only once a week at Mrs. Richard's Dance Academy.

In order to learn ballroom dancing at the academy, all sixth-grade boys were required to wear a jacket, tie, dress shoes, and white gloves. Girls wore dresses, dance shoes, white gloves, and bows in their hair.

Joanne wore a scarlet dress with a matching red bow strategically placed on the side of her golden hair. We always chose each other as partners.

Elizabeth, another girl I knew, also attended Berkeley Academy, was twelve years old and Joanne's classmate. Her parents were good friends with mine and attended the same church as we did. Elizabeth, taller and thinner than Joanne, had dark mousy hair and sad green eyes. She didn't smile much, and her eyes never sparkled like Joanne's. When we met at church or she accompanied her parents to dinner at our house, I never spoke to her. Instead, I watched TV and ignored her. Elizabeth could not compare to Joanne.

That fall, Berkeley hosted a harvest festival Sadie-Hawkins dance, and the girls could invite whomever they wanted. All the kids from our dance class planned to go and were practicing their steps. Every evening, I waited near the phone, convinced that Joanne would call. By the Monday before the dance, I began to worry she wouldn't call, but I knew from asking friends she had not yet invited anyone else.

Monday evening, I got a call from Elizabeth. Her soft and hesitant voice came through the phone line. "Tom, do you want to go to the Sadie-Hawkins with me?" My throat tightened, and I wanted to tell her I already had a date. It wouldn't be a lie since I was just waiting for Joanne's invitation. Instead, knowing my mother insisted on making all those decisions for me, I said, "Let me ask my parents." Putting the phone on our small rectangular living room table, I walked into the kitchen. I told Mom about Elizabeth's invitation and that I was waiting for Joanne to call. "Tom, you know what's right," she said. "You have to go with the person who asks you first. Tell Elizabeth you would love to go with her. Dad and I will drive the two of you to the dance."

"But Mom," I replied, "I know Joanne will call soon. I want to go with her." Mom just shook her head and motioned for me to return to the phone. In resignation, I slowly walked back to the living room and picked up the phone. Struggling to maintain my composure, I said, "Sure, I'd love to go with you."

She said quietly, "That's great, Tom," but I could sense how happy she was. She didn't know any other boys, and she attended an all-girls school. Her parents refused to let her go to a dance academy, and she sat with them at church and spoke with no one.

Later that night, Joanne called and I had to tell her I already had a date. I had never been so miserable and was sure she thought I didn't want to go with her. I couldn't even watch the thirty minutes of TV I was allowed on school nights and simply stared at the wall until Mom came in and told me to turn off the lights. She obviously knew I was unhappy but simply said, "You did the right thing."

The night of the dance, my parents drove me to Elizabeth's house, I gave her the corsage my mother had bought at a nearby flower shop, and then mom and dad took us to Berkeley. When we arrived, they said, "Have fun. We'll be back at eleven o'clock," and drove away.

As Elizabeth and I walked into the school auditorium, Joanne was dancing with her date, a short quiet boy with glasses whom I recognized from the dance school. She was wearing that same red dress and her blond hair caught the light from the crystal chandelier hanging from the ceiling. My stomach churned, I felt nauseous, and I hoped that eleven o'clock would arrive soon.

The music had stopped, and when it began to play again,

I invited Elizabeth to dance. We started to move around the floor. "Sorry," Elizabeth said as she continuously stepped on my feet, and then again "Sorry, sorry, sorry." Her face became flushed and her eyes seemed to moisten. I tried not to look annoyed. It was too obvious she had never learned to dance. After moving in silence, and dragging our feet across the floor, we finally gave up and decided to sit.

Midway through the never-ending evening, Elizabeth turned pale and ran to the bathroom. When she had not returned after fifteen minutes, I went in search and found her coming out of the girl's bathroom, accompanied by two female teachers. Elizabeth's eyes were puffy as if she had been crying and her pale face had turned white. I heard the teacher who had her arm around Elizabeth say, "Don't worry. It's a normal part of life. You'll be fine."

Suddenly I forgot how miserable I was. Elizabeth seemed so fragile and scared. Awkwardly I took her hand, and we slowly walked back to the auditorium where we sat side by side and drank our Cokes. I asked her if she was feeling better, and when she nodded, I tried to find something to say. Finally, I blurted out, "Do you like science fiction?"

"I like Ray Bradbury," she answered. "He's very deep. And I like Van Vogt's *Slan.* It's so sad. The telepaths get persecuted because they're different and people fear them."

How could she have known that Bradbury was my favorite author ever since I had read the *Martian Chronicles?* I was a lifetime member of the "Science Fiction Book Club" which sent me two books or anthologies every month.

I don't know why, but I felt comfortable with her and revealed a secret even my parents didn't know. "Sometimes when we play football in gym class, the coach throws me the ball. Then he yells for everyone to tackle me and pile on top. He singles out those of us who don't like football. I guess, when you're different, people don't always treat you nicely. I wish I lived in another universe where people had special powers. I would never be piled on. If we all had telepathic powers, we wouldn't need to talk at all."

Elizabeth smiled and murmured her agreement. "Maybe we would understand each other better."

Soon Elizabeth felt well enough to return to the dance floor. I don't remember her stepping on my feet this time, and we seemed to glide across the floor. The lights flashed. It was eleven o'clock and time to leave.

My parents were waiting outside, and as we drove her home, I glanced over at Elizabeth. Her face had regained its normal color. I had never realized how the green in her eyes was full of specs of brown. They seemed to dance. When I walked her to the door, she said quietly, "Thanks Tom, I had a really great evening."

The next morning, when I went downstairs, Mom was making breakfast. Bacon sizzled in a frying pan she had placed on the gas oven. It smelled delicious. She removed the strips, put them on my plate, and emptied the fat into an aluminum can. Mom used her fork to whip the eggs and milk mixture she had ready in a glass bowl and poured it into the empty pan.

"Elizabeth's mom called," she said. "She told me Elizabeth had a problem at the dance and you were really helpful. The poor thing was scared to death and ran to the bathroom."

"I forgot to tell you about that," I said. "She got sick but then was better and we even danced again. Was it something she ate?"

Mom looked at me, "It's a natural thing that happens to girls at her age. She's fine now. I don't think her parents ever talked with her about some of the facts of life, so she didn't know what was happening."

"Mom," I said, "I'm glad I took Elizabeth."

Mom just smiled and pushed a strand of hair out of her eyes. "I know," she said and continued to stir the scrambled eggs before adding them to the pieces of bacon on my plate.

2
JEANNIE WITH THE
LIGHT BROWN HAIR

THE SUMMER OF 1961 WAS going to be different. We filed away the unpleasant memories of previous summers of boy's camp; of baseball and bullies, canoeing and camp cliques, food fights and football, but most of all, summers without girls. We were long past the childish days of riding bikes and attending all-boy events and looking forward to driving ourselves to dances with girls.

My best friend, Charles Shalmas, was playing a Chopin piece on the baby grand piano in his parent's living room in their home in Bay Ridge, Brooklyn. His cousin Nick and I sat on the flowered sofa while I inspected the Lebanese knickknacks Charles's father had placed on the coffee table. A specific one intrigued me. It was a triangle-like amulet with a symbol representing the Phoenician goddess Tanit, the mother of creation. At least that's what Charles told me.

The amulet had a circular head, two stick arms, and a triangle body. It looked very similar to the ancient Egyptian symbol of eternal life I had read about in one of my National Geographic magazines.

Charles, Nick, and I were close friends who got along well, despite our marked differences. Charles—short and fat with a hooked nose and curly sandy hair—loved classical music, philosophy, and discussing religion. He was a straight-A student at the prep school we both attended. Nick was from Queens, where he and his parents lived in a brownstone tenement. He was tall, skinny, and a "natural" at most sports. Nick attended public school, and reading and studying were not his forte. He loved sports, most of all football and baseball. I was average height with short-cropped hair and apple cheeks. People said I had sparkling brown eyes. Unlike Charles, I worked hard to achieve the grades that he received without effort. I acted as the bridge between the two of them, as I was equally happy watching sports or listening to a classical concert.

While Charles played, I became lost in my memories of the previous winter. Nick, Charles, and I had gone to one of the local parks. After an hour, Nick left. The weather had grown too cold to play baseball, and he decided to take the subway home to Queens and watch sports on TV. I was bored, so I hit Charles with well-packed snowball. "Stop it!" he said. Then I hit him again, and as I ran away, I slipped and fell. Before I could get up, he sat on me, and with his full weight on my chest, I couldn't move.

"Let me up," I said, "I'm freezing!"

"Not till you promise to stop."

It took a full thirty minutes before I gave in. Later, Nick laughingly told me Charles would have never sat on him, as he never would have been clumsy and tripped.

I returned to the present and woke from my reverie when Charles stopped playing and said, "Let's go to Pennsylvania for a week. My dad found the perfect place. It's an inn on a farm near Lancaster. It will be better than the last two summers we spent at that boys' camp in the Poconos." I had never heard of Lancaster but if the other two were going, I was in. At first, my parents were unsure and asked many questions. Mr. Shalmas insisted he knew the owners of the place and convinced Mom and Dad that three boys could not get into much trouble at a farm in the Pennsylvania countryside. At least not in only one week. Things were different in those days.

Mr. Shalmas, a pleasant portly man with a Havana cigar stuck permanently in his mouth, was a successful businessman. He carried a big wad of one, five, and ten-dollar bills in a sterling silver money clip. When he took us for ice cream or hot dogs, he would always pay, rolling out the crisp new bills with his pudgy fingers. He owned a fabric business in Beirut, but the civil unrest in Lebanon had gotten worse and had not been good for the textile industry, causing him to switch his business to importing dates, pistachios, and dried fruits. He sold these in his neighborhood store in Bay Ridge.

In those days, Bay Ridge was a tree-lined suburban section of Brooklyn. Charles and I attended Poly Prep, an all boy's school with a long, winding drive passing two ponds and ending at a magnificent stone structure, the school's main building. Years later, the city destroyed the ponds and surrounding grounds to make an access road for the new Verrazano Bridge.

The three of us left Bay Ridge in Mr. Shalmas' Cadillac, on a Saturday in June 1961. Mr. Shalmas was at the wheel, the signature cigar unlit in his mouth. It was a half-day's trip from Brooklyn to Intercourse near Lancaster in the Pennsylvania Dutch countryside. The route rambled through small towns, some with just a few buildings, others with churches, town halls, and main streets with traffic lights.

To pass the time, I listened to Cousin Brucie on my transistor radio. He played the latest rock-and-roll songs from the 1961 hit parade. "Turn off that noise!" Charles said. "I'm trying to study this piece of music!" Charles was a trained classical pianist, who even at twelve showed signs of a promising future.

"Stuff it, Charles!" Nick replied.

Nick, with his nasal Flatbush accent and his slicked-back hair, shared my appreciation for 1950s rock-and-roll. He also shared my interest in tennis, and we looked forward to a week of playing. When we mentioned our plans to Charles, he replied with a somewhat disdainful air, "I can't play tennis; I could sprain a piano finger, and then what would I do?"

We got to the Inn, whose name I now forget, late Sunday afternoon. After Mr. Shalmas dropped us off, I discovered that the other two would bunk together at one end of the boarding house, and I would be alone at the other. I remember walking down a long, narrow corridor from the busy front of the building to an isolated room at the back. I was not used to being by myself, since at summer camp the cabins held several bunk beds for kids and a counselor.

The first day, Nick and I decided to let Charles practice piano and went off to play tennis and then explore the farm. It was a functioning farm with cows, chickens, horses, and some goats and fields of wheat, hay, and barley. Besides the tennis courts, the inn also had a pool.

We all got together for lunch in the inn's spacious dining room. Some high school girls, working as waitresses for the summer months, served lunch. Two of the girls, who were going to be high school sophomores, inquired about New York once they found out we lived there. Jeannie, a girl with light brown hair, cute nose, welcoming smile, big blue eyes, and tan legs, moved with athletic grace as she carried our lunch plates. With her developed breasts, I saw Jeannie as a "woman," not like the "girls" I met at my prep school's white-gloved dances. I soon learned Jeannie could wait tables in the summer, drive a tractor the rest of the year, and still be on the high school cheerleading squad. That night, I dreamed of "Jeannie with the light brown hair," or maybe it was the goddess Tanit in my dream. It all got mixed up in my head, first Jeannie then Tanit then Jeannie again.

At breakfast on Wednesday morning, while we waited for the girls to take our order, Nick whispered, "I'm going to ask these girls if we can all go to the movies."

I whispered back, "They'll never go out with us. Charles and I are thirteen and you're only fourteen. All three of them are going to be sophomores in high school."

Charles overheard our whispers and opined in a loud voice, "Who cares about girls, anyway. I need to go to bed early and I don't watch movies." Fortunately, no one beyond our table heard him.

Along with two others whose nametags said Barb and Helen, Jeannie came over and took our breakfast orders. She introduced us to Barb, whom we had not met and said that she was "in training."

Charles ate oatmeal; I had scrambled eggs, bacon, and toast, and Nick chose pancakes with sausages. After the girls returned with our orders, Nick ventured, "You girls want to take in a movie Friday night?"

Surprisingly, they said, "Yes." Maybe it was because Nick smoked cigarettes, carried a switchblade, and wore a leather jacket, or maybe because he made sure that a condom (his only one) fell out of his pocket and onto the floor while the girls placed the breakfast dishes on the table.

Jeannie looked at me. "Are you coming too?"

"You bet," I replied. "What's playing?"

She smiled, and I became lost in those blue eyes that looked like pools of cool water on a hot day. "I think a beach movie is playing at the drive-in. We'll bring the soda pop," she said.

On Friday night, Jeannie drove us to the movie in her 1955 Buick. Charles ended up coming anyway, and I was wedged between Jeannie and Charles in the front seat. Nick sat in the back with Barb and Helen. Honestly, I don't remember anything about Barb and Helen, but I do remember Jeannie's lilac perfume, and the way it made me dizzy and happy all at the same time.

The movie was a beach flick where boy and girl got together, broke up, and then made up again, with a lot of singing in between. After we arrived back at the inn, we made root beer floats with vanilla ice cream from the kitchen's large fridge, sat on the lawn in front of the building, and looked at the night stars. With no large buildings around, they shone brightly against the dark sky. I put my arm around Jeannie and we kissed, my first. It was just one short kiss, but I remember she tasted like strawberries. We didn't say anything, but at that moment, I fell madly in love.

The next day, Mr. Shalmas arrived. "How was your week?" he asked. "Fine," we all answered before getting into the car for the trip home. I later learned that Mr. Shalmas had paid for a good part of my stay and that is why my parents had agreed to let me go so readily. Jeannie and I promised to write. I waited for a letter that never came. Still, I will be eternally grateful to her for my first kiss.

That summer ended too soon and school began again. During the school year, I saw Nick only sporadically. When we met, we didn't have much to talk about. He still didn't like school while I remained submerged in schoolwork. Charles and I shared many of the same classes and studied together on weekends. That year I turned fourteen and Charles attended my birthday party. Nick had a baseball game and couldn't come.

The summer of 1962, my father's company transferred him to New Jersey, and we left Bay Ridge. Since I stayed busy packing for the move and preparing for my new school, I had no time to spend with Nick or Charles. I later heard they went back to Pennsylvania and spent another week at the farm but did not see Jeannie. She had moved on.

Charles and I kept in touch until we both went off to college in the late sixties. He attended Yale University on a music scholarship. Sometime later, he wrote me that Nick had failed his senior year of high school and repeated a year. Later, he informed me that Nick had been arrested for shoplifting and dropped out of school before graduating.

In 1975, my mother got a Christmas card from Mrs. Shalmas. She wrote that her husband, Mr. Shalmas, had died that year of a heart attack and Charles had gone to Beirut, Lebanon to salvage what was left of the family textile business. The following year, Mrs. Shalmas died. My mother saw her obituary in a local Brooklyn newspaper, which a mutual friend sent her. I guess she could not live without her husband. I never heard from Charles again.

The Lebanese civil war started in 1975. It ended fifteen years later in 1990. Civilian deaths totaled 250,000 during the conflict. I still wonder if Charles was one of them.

3
SLUTTY PUTTY

IT WAS 1962, MY SOPHOMORE year at Morrisdale High School. I was new in town. Sally Puttmore, from my new church's Sunday school class, had invited me to the Sophomore Fall Sock Hop. She knew I had attended an exclusive prep school in Manhattan through freshman year, and I guess Sally thought it was cool to be on a date with someone from the "city," as everyone called New York.

The night of the dance was unseasonably warm. We met in the high school parking lot, and Sally gasped in surprise when I arrived dressed in light blue shorts and matching knee socks. For some reason, my parents suggested the outfit. I didn't know then that you should never trust your parents' advice, at least when it came to clothing.

Sally's black leather jacket, matching boots, and tight black jeans offset her midnight eyes and raven hair. A low-cut silk blouse showed off her nipples, and her jeans stretched over her rear, revealing every line and curve, as well as the switchblade in her front side pocket. "My Dad allows me to have it for protection," she said. I remember fantasizing about kissing her goodnight after the dance.

As we walked into the school gym, I noticed the other boys wore blue jeans and flannel shirts. The girls, except those in Sally's crowd, dressed in short cheerleader-type pleated dresses and penny loafers. Sally's friends chose their own uniform that resembled hers: black leather jackets, tight jeans, and boots.

At the time, I thought Sally's friends a strange mix. Some looked like the tough gang members out of the James Dean movie *Rebel without a Cause* and others like the James Dean character or the character's friend, the self-designated intellectual. Sally was a mix of both.

Sandy-haired Harry, a junior, carried a whiskey flask that was always full. He loved to brag about the fast cars he drove. His standard line, "I only drink whiskey; beer is for jocks and babies," was followed by a loud laugh, but his blue eyes betrayed hidden pain. Madge, a tall, short-haired sophomore, wore horn-rimmed glasses and chain-smoked the filtered cigarettes she retrieved from the black leather shoulder bag where she also kept the books her parents forbade her to read. Troy had long black hair, a dark beard, and a tattoo of a naked woman on his right arm. He had dropped out of high school and worked as an auto mechanic. He had parked his Harley nearby. Under his black leather jacket, he wore a white t-shirt with one sleeve rolled up so he could place a packet of Marlboros in the upturned fold.

After introducing me to her friends, Sally asked Madge

about the copy of *Tropic of Capricorn* which had fallen out of her purse. Madge replied, "It's better than *Catcher*." I soon learned that Sally loved Holden Caulfield in the *Catcher* book when she quoted his words, "High school is full of phonies, who keep making believe they give a damn if the football team loses, and all you do is talk about girls and liquor and sex all day, and everybody sticks together in these dirty little goddam cliques." She then added, "These stupid football jocks are going nowhere and will never accomplish anything beyond high school."

Sally had previously told me her father was a Yale-educated physicist and a direct descendent of the Pilgrims. Her mother, who had gone to Vassar, was a member of the *Daughters of the American Revolution*. They were like most of Morrisdale's upper-class parents. They took their kids to Broadway shows, concerts at the Met, and museums in New York, their "cultural oasis."

After I turned down both a whiskey and a beer, and my attempt at dancing was less than successful, Sally decided we should leave. When she started adjusting that silk shirt, revealing more of what was underneath, I agreed to go. I was too young to drive, so we began walking to her home. A 1957 cherry-colored Chevy Belair convertible with silver chrome hubcaps and white wings pulled up beside us. Harry was behind the wheel. The car seemed new because after totally rebuilding the engine, he had recently painted it himself. "Let's go for a spin," he said. "We can drive against traffic on the Boulevard and play chicken, or do Chinese fire drills in downtown Denville."

"What's a Chinese fire drill?" I asked.

Harry smiled in disbelief. "You never heard of it? You

know. It's when we stop at a light, we all run around the car before the light changes, and we switch drivers. If the cops come, I've got a supercharged V-8 underneath the hood of this beauty. They'll never catch us."

Sally was in the car in a second. "I think I'll pass on this one," I said. "It's almost eleven and I have church tomorrow." I could tell she was again disappointed in me. She pulled off her jacket and laid it on the seat as Harry revved the engine. I could see the erect nipples under her silk blouse.

Harry said, "Suit yourself," and shifted into first gear.

Sally quipped, "Have fun in Sunday school!"

Off they raced, looking for something to make the night different. I walked the three miles back home. My parents were waiting up and Mom asked, "How was the dance? I didn't hear a car. I thought Dr. Puttmore was going to drive you home afterward?"

"Fine," I replied and went straight to my room.

Mondays, I had gym second period. It was a brisk, sunny fall day so the coach sent us outside to play soccer. As the period was almost ending, we retired to the locker room and warm showers. We all walked into the showers, and I looked around at a bunch of circumcised athletes. I quickly turned to face the shower wall.

There were no blacks, no Jews, and few Italians in Morrisdale in those days. My Italian background was just one more way I was different from the others. No one noticed as I quickly showered and wrapped a towel around my waist. Several of the jocks crowded around. A blond burley senior named Tom, the halfback for the football team, punched me softly on the shoulder and asked, "You and 'Slutty Putty' left the dance early. So how was she? What did you get off her?" My puzzled look betrayed me.

"Aw," Tom said. "He don't even know what we're talking about. He didn't get nothing off her."

The school administration had not yet turned on the heat in the locker room, and the room had just gotten colder. As the crowd drifted away, another jock named Nick, called out, "Next time leave her to me. At least, I know what to do."

A third voice chimed in, "Yah, but you're too stupid for her. She's a brainy slut." Left alone in the shower room with my towel still draped around my waist, I knew I had just become a nobody in their eyes.

Several days later, I stood in the lunch line behind a football player named Paul. He made some comment and when I came back with a smart-aleck retort, he punched me in the stomach. I should have taken my empty tray and smashed it across his face, but I did nothing. He laughed, put a burger and fries on his tray, and moved on without looking back. I told myself I was not a violent guy and justified my lack of response. But what type of person was I?

I didn't see much of Sally that sophomore year, nor the junior year that followed. I was not in her crowd, nor was I a jock. I soldiered on, trying to find myself and overcome the deathblow to my reputation by joining the hockey team and trying to get invited to parties. I had never wanted to be a jock or a *player*, so that did not work out so well.

Two years later, when we were seniors, Sally and I found ourselves working on a history project together. It was about religion in early America. I still don't know why she picked that topic, but she and I were the only two who did. We became friends and eventually received an "A" for the project. By then, she had dropped the fast cars, the switchblade, and cigarettes, but still drank Jim Beam whiskey and was now dating a junior named Henry who was top student in his class. Everyone, including his and her parents, said he was "Harvard material." The parents did not know, or did not care to know, what everyone at school knew. A senior who worked part-time at the local pharmacy told us all that Henry would come in often and buy packs and packs of condoms. Large size.

Sally had become an agnostic. She didn't rule out God, she just couldn't believe in him, and she found the virgin birth laughable. She never showed up at church, even on Easter morning or Christmas, but she loved our discussions on philosophy. At some point, she began to consider me her intellectual equal. Although with Sally, everything was an intellectual exercise, I never gave up trying to make her see that religion was something to practice, not debate. For her, it was always about sharpening the mind.

By graduation, she had not changed her low opinion of the school jocks. They still ridiculed her, referring to her "junior" boyfriend, the large condoms, and all the rest. It was a sort of standoff. They courted popularity and prowess at sports. She obsessed over her future and Ivy League colleges.

I could never reconcile *Sally the intellectual* with *Sally the sexual*. Maybe they were both part of her rebellion against what she considered a boring, suburban mid-1960s lifestyle.

Vassar accepted Sally in the spring of our senior year.

Later, while attending college, she met John, a student at Yale. They married, he became a writer and she a professor of literature. Sally and I wrote to each other from time to time but neither of us went back to class reunions. After John died, Sally returned to Morrisdale for our 30th class reunion. I passed on the occasion but felt bad about missing the opportunity to see her again. Her husband had not found a publisher for his only book. She tried unsuccessfully for several years to get it published, and then became a successful writer, herself.

These days, I lie in bed at night and wonder what she writes. Does she write romantic fiction, memories, or discourses on social issues?

Unlike in my high school years, I now believe that most things in life are gray. There is no black or white. Sally and the jocks looked down on each other. They probably took offense at the fact that she would never sleep with them. Her independence and intellect threatened them. She saw them as without a future because they could not see beyond high school. Maybe she can see them as I do now, a group of insecure boys searching for who they were. And just maybe, they too were able to make something of themselves.

4

THE YEARBOOK

EARLY IN THE MORNING ON the day before graduation, I sat at my desk in homeroom. My senior yearbook lay open on the table in front of me. Several friends had just stopped by to sign under their pictures. I looked up and gasped. Ron Black was approaching. Ron had not spoken to me in almost two years, and I wondered what he wanted now.

Like a used car salesman who wanted to close a deal but did not want to appear anxious, Ron sauntered over to my desk. As his five-foot-ten-inch frame hovered over me, he said, "Hey pardner, I wanna sign your yearbook." He always called me "pardner" instead of my real name. He pronounced it with a Texas twang. Ron still had his wavy black hair cut in the same short-in-the-back style and the front was slicked back with Brylcreem. Somewhat taken aback, I looked up. What would he write?

It all started in the fall of 1962, our sophomore year. Ron and I were both transfer students at Morrisdale High School. He was from Lubbock, Texas, and I was from Brooklyn, New York. The other one hundred students in our class had attended grammar school, junior high and now high school together. On our first day, one of the cheerleaders looked at Ron and me and asked, "Where in the world are you two from?" Ron's Texas drawl, leather cowboy boots, and bolo tie made it seem like he was getting ready to ride in a rodeo. With my short sleeve white shirt and prep school tie with school emblem on the front, I also looked out of place. That day, "Texas Ron" and I became friends.

Soon Ron dropped the boots and tie. My parents claimed they could not afford other clothes. Ron told me, "Loosen up, pardner. No chick wants to go out with a guy who wears a logo tie to school." I abandoned the tie but kept the white shirts.

Ron convinced me to participate in debate. He joined the team first and made sure I was accepted. Debate, though Ron loved it, was not, in his words, a "chick- pleaser." Ron told me, "Chicks love hockey and football players. Too bad I can't skate, and I'm not into catching a ball or getting hit by big muscular types."

Though I couldn't skate either, I decided to join the ice hockey club. We were not an official school team, but played against prep schools that had their own indoor ice rinks. I specialized in falling in front of opposing team players. They either became entangled in my skates and fell, or lost the puck when they tried to skate around my sprawled body.

Our club could not afford to buy time at a local ice rink more than once a week, so we practiced on lakes and ponds. One of the ponds was just below a hill where Ron's parents had purchased a large six-bedroom house.

We set up pieces of plywood as sideboards for a makeshift rink. Ron came down to the pond when the ice was thick and watched us practice. He laughed when I fell, but he always shouted out my name as if he were cheering a rider at a Texas rodeo.

Home games were on Sundays at six in the morning at the only public rink near Morrisdale. Most of us just stayed up all night and then played. On occasion, a player or two arrived having had one too many beers. Ron never made it to watch an early morning game. He would say, "Pardner, I gotta get my beauty sleep for the chicks, and besides, I like to party till four and then hit the hay."

On occasion, Ron invited me over for a snack at his house after hockey practice. He never invited the others as we would practice our debate techniques. During one session, Ron told me, "This is not poetry recitation. Go after your opponent! Yah gotta be in their face. Challenge their argument point-by point!" I tried but I was not Ron. He would slap me on the back and say, "That's okay, pardner. You do great at the poetry recitations."

After seven months, we still hadn't gotten any dates. Ron asked out most of the cheerleaders but had no takers. They dated guys who had graduated from Morrisdale and were in college or current members of the football team.

In order to improve his popularity, Ron decided to throw a party in February and invite both the sophomore and junior classes. His parents were out of town, and he had stolen the key to their liquor cabinet. The party livened up after Ron brought out the liquor from his father's stock. He seemed to be in his element, and the popular girls actually spoke to him.

Even Bobby Underwool, the sophomore class geek, showed up. As the evening progressed, some of the football players got drunk, began arm wrestling in the living room and then tore off their t-shirts to flex their muscles. Two of them pulled down Bobby's pants and removed his under shorts. The jocks wadded them together and began to throw them around like a floppy football. Bobby chased them with one hand over his groin and the other trying to intercept the pass. I moved out of target range and into the kitchen where it was safer.

As I watched from the kitchen, I felt sorry for Bobby and thought, *If those were my underpants and I was running around naked in front of half the upper-school girls, I would want someone to help me.* I really did not want to go back into the living room and draw attention to myself. Yes, I played hockey, but they still did not consider me as one of them.

With some trepidation, I returned to the room and helped Bobby retrieve his clothes, which lay scattered all over. With tears welling in his eyes, he said, "Thanks," and quickly ran out the front door. The two ringleaders saw Bobby leave and sent him off with laughter and jeers. They stood at the door and watched him as he hopped out to the street, trying to pull up his pants as he moved. The boys' laughter followed him as he ran down the silent street past the dark houses.

I went outside to clear my head, and when I returned to

the living room, it seemed like all the others had paired off and were making out. Some of the cheerleaders disappeared to rooms upstairs with their boyfriends. The rhythmic noise of a creaky bed descended from the floor above. Although it was only ten p.m. and my parents wouldn't pick me up till eleven-thirty, I decided to walk home. The air smelled like decaying leaves, and I picked up my pace as the crisp winter cold began to seep through my jacket.

As I walked in the door, my mom heard me and said, "You're home early. Didn't like the party?"

I mumbled something, took a frozen coke out of the fridge, went up to my room and fell on my bed. Unlike Texas Ron, I didn't have a stack of *Playboy* magazines stashed under the mattress. I turned on the radio and tried to sleep, but continued to see Bobby running around naked trying to retrieve his pants. I couldn't get out of my head the mocking laughter that followed him down the street.

On Monday, Ron stopped by my homeroom just before the first bell rang. He looked worn out from the weekend. "Hey pardner, why'd yah leave so early? I missed yah. The girls were just getting loosened up. Yah might have gotten to first or even second base. I got so wasted I don't remember what base I got to."

"Ron," I snapped, "I don't drink liquor, and I don't enjoy watching people make asses out of themselves. Look what happened to Bobby!"

Ron looked at me. His eyes narrowed and his nose turned up. Then he said, "Pardner, ya betta start drinkin' if you want to be popular like me. Besides, what's a party without half nekkid girls and booze?"

Ron became an overnight hit with the girls, at least for

a couple of weeks. Then life returned to normal. Ron was still Ron. He didn't play football, was only a sophomore, and hadn't grown up in Morrisdale.

In March, our debate team attended a tournament at Temple University in Philadelphia. Mr. Thomas, our high school history teacher and debate coach, took the six of us on the school bus, stuck us in rooms at the Howard Johnson's motel, and went off to dinner with his cousin who lived somewhere in the suburbs. Since we were the only male sophomores, Thomas put Ron and me together in a hotel room.

The debate topic was "state's rights vs. the rights of the Federal Government." We had to defend the pro-Federal government viewpoint, which meant more federal power. An excellent debater, Ron was part of the three-man team. Mr. Thomas chose him as the second debater following a junior and before a senior. The senior would do the final rebuttal and make our closing statement.

I was on the backup team. Mr. Thomas told me, "Be ready if needed." The other two members were Randy Williams, a quiet sophomore, and Sally Smythe, a popular junior who was dating a senior. I really didn't know Randy, but he seemed to view everything with a somewhat critical eye. However, I liked Sally. She had been kind and showed me the ropes when I first joined the debate team. She always seemed in control and was not easily ruffled, even during a difficult debate.

During dinner at a local burger joint, Ron kept nervously running his fingers through his greasy black hair. Sally tried to put him at ease by complimenting how he had done in our practice session back home. I also wanted to make Ron feel better about the next day.

"Relax," I said, "You'll be fine."

"I will be once I get some liquid courage," Ron answered.

After dinner, I walked back to the hotel with Sally and Randy and then went to my room to study our tactics for the next day. Ron hit a local liquor store. He used his fake I.D. and returned to the room with two large bottles of whiskey. He then walked down the hallway offering drinks to the others.

"Don't let Mr. Thomas catch you with those bottles, Ron," I said.

He replied, "Keep this to yourself, pardner."

Back in our room, he offered me a whiskey. "It will make you feel good about tomorrow," he said. When I turned it down, he added, "Suit yourself," drank half the bottle, and passed out on his bed.

The next morning, I helped him into a cold shower and got some coffee into him. Ron had recovered by debate time and performed well. We lost by just a few points to a more experienced Pennsylvania team.

On the Tuesday after we returned to school, the principal put Ron on a three-day suspension, and Mr. Thomas dropped him from the debate team. That was the last time Ron ever spoke to me. I was puzzled and hurt by his changed behavior. Shortly after Ron returned from his suspension, Sally Smythe asked me, "What's up between you and Ron? You were such great friends."

"Sometimes friendships turn out differently than you think," I said, "but I don't know what's up with Ron."

For the rest of the year, in the cafeteria or halls, when he was talking up some of the girls, he would look at me and glare. I would hear him telling them about what an "asshole" I was. When he passed around invitations to parties at his home, I was never invited. The parties, however, still did not win him any real friends.

I finally figured it out. Ron blamed me for his suspension. He knew I did not like drinking. I had been quite clear on that, so he thought I had reported his drinking. Ron had told me that night in the hotel to keep the drinking episode to myself. I did, but someone else didn't. I don't know why Ron didn't confront me, given our friendship and his in-your-face personality, I would have told him, it was not my style to rat out a friend. Why hadn't he trusted me? His verdict was in. "Guilty as charged." After a few months, everyone forgot the incident except Texas Ron.

My senior year things changed. I discovered if you are willing to help people, prepping them for exams and helping with their homework, you can make friends, even among those so-called "popular" girls. During study hall period, I would get a pass to the library where I liked to read. As I was good in French and History, cheerleaders, like red-haired and hazel-eyed Maureen, blonde and blue-eyed Jenny, and raven-haired Bonnie, would ask me for help with their homework. I never got a date with any of them; they all had boyfriends in college. But we became friends. When they asked me to invite Gail White, a senior who didn't have a date, to the senior prom, I agreed. She was a sweet girl but not particularly attractive. Ron took a pretty girl, a petit sophomore. She acted as if she was in heaven, and Ron showed her off like a trophy.

The last day of school, Gail White wrote something nice about our date in my yearbook. One of the cheerleaders, with whom I joked around, authored the caption placed under my yearbook picture. It said, "Wants to join the Foreign Service. Probably will join the Foreign Legion."

So why, almost two years later, did Ron Black want to sign my yearbook? As Ron looked down at me, he said, "Pardner, I just found out last night that it was Randy Williams who sold me out. He told Mr. Thomas about the liquor."

I nodded. "I thought we were friends."

"I know it," he said. "Just let me sign the damn book."

Ron took the book, wrote a few words below his picture, and handed it back to me. Then he said, "Good luck at college next year. I've always envied your success with the girls." He moved on, trying to intercept two cheerleaders, but they saw him coming and fled. I couldn't help feeling sorry for Ron. He never succeeded in becoming the popular guy he wanted to be.

As I looked down at the open yearbook, I saw that he had written just seven words. "I like your style pardner, don't change."

When we were sophomores, I would have cherished the words. But I no longer needed Ron's approval.

5

THAT MATCH

"YOU KNOW, BILLY," I SAID, "I can't forget my match last spring against that player from Greenhill."

We were sitting at Paul's Family Diner. Usually after tennis practice, Billy and I went to Paul's, where we drank root beer floats and ate burgers. The diner was almost empty as the "five o'clock special" crowd had just begun to arrive.

Located in the same spot off Route 46 since the fifties, the diner was a favorite of athletic teams from the neighboring towns. It had windows facing the highway, two rows of tables, and a counter with a cash register at one end. Chrome swivel stools with maroon-colored seats were placed strategically along the counter. The waitresses, mostly high school kids working after school, hung out at one end of the counter when they were not serving and gossiped about their boyfriends. Paul, the owner, sat at the entrance, underneath a showcase with a baseball from the

1956 World Series, signed by the entire New York Yankees team.

Billy Buller, my best friend, stood six-foot-two inches, had a booming serve and arms long enough to cover any shot at the net. He wore horn-rimmed glasses for distance and had short sandy hair, cut at the ears. Only five-nine, I envied his serve and reach but made up for my deficiencies with quick reflexes. Billy and I both hit the stuffing out of the ball and played only serve and volley tennis. Maybe that's why we ended up as doubles partners.

Putting down his root beer float, Billy handed me a napkin, indicated the catsup mark on my cheek and said, "Yeah, I remember that match. You played fifth position, last match of the day, and we were all sure you'd beat that guy."

I grumbled, "I played real well the first set. Things were going great. Then the wind came up."

Soft peddling his response, Billy commented, "You kinda let the wind get to you."

The two of us loved tennis, but we were very different in our emotional approach to the sport. He could screw up royally, get mad at himself or his opponent, and still play his best. Not me. Coach Johnson always told me, "Focus on the ball and get out of your head, block out those negative emotions. Don't be so afraid to lose. Be the ball. Focus on the seams of the ball as it turns in flight." In spite of his advice, if my opponent got to me or rattled my cage, or weather conditions were not perfect, my game turned to crap.

My mom, who read the Bible a lot, had another approach. She would just say, "Pride cometh before a fall." She knew

I hated to lose to those who didn't hit the ball clean and hard. My idols were Australian tennis star John Newcomb and American Arthur Ashe. I tried hard, maybe too hard.

Tennis always seemed to be about masculinity; like who had the biggest racquet. You had to hit the ball as hard as possible and rush the net like a soldier attacking the enemy lines, and losing was never an option. I remember clearly that self-imposed pressure to win.

As the diner began to fill up, I put down my hamburger. My stomach tightened. "Greenwood High had lost most of their matches up to that point, and we thought it would go really fast. I played against that pudgy guy with the bush haircut and short, fat legs. He could barely get to the ball. If I hit it wide, it was out of his reach. He also thought he was hot shit and took a bow each time he won a point."

As we talked, my mind jumped back to that day. "It was so hot, my hair was plastered to my forehead with sweat," I said, "and I had to keep pushing it out of my eyes. My arms were coated with a greasy mixture of sweat and suntan lotion, and I kept toweling off my right hand so I could grasp my racquet.

"I got real pissed off after the first set, when the sun went down and it got windy. You know the wind screws with my ball toss."

Billy was sympathetic. "I remember watching from the benches at court side. Set one, your pudgy opponent's serve had some pace but bounced too high to your forehand, making it easy to return. You put all his serves away for winners. You were also booming in plenty of aces, hitting the lines regularly with your serve. After you won so easily, six games to zero, I decided to go and watch another match.

When I returned I saw that it had all changed." He shook his head.

The waitress came by to see if we needed anything else. I told her, "No, thanks." Then I looked at Billy, who was wolfing down his cheeseburger, and retorted, "Things really did change in the second set. My opponent's lobs swirled in the wind and kept me away from the net. I couldn't volley, take the ball in the air or quickly end the point. The wind slowed down his serve, made it drift sideways. Without its former pace, I had trouble returning the ball. I blew most of my returns out, over the baseline. I think he was specifically hitting junk balls to get to me. When I put the ball over the line, he would smirk and take a bow. I wanted to break my racquet over his head. Within twenty minutes, I lost that set six games to four. It got colder. Before set three, I needed time to think. So I marched over to the sidelines and pulled on my hoodie."

Billy laughed. "I haven't seen you wear your hoodie since that match. Coach called you a hot potato because you handled volleys at the net like hot potatoes and slammed them back for winners. I remember you had the word 'potato' inscribed on it. Your reflexes have always been one of your best attributes."

"You probably know what I was thinking. I told myself that I was playing like a potato-head not a hot potato, and I was dropping the match to a real loser. In anger, I threw my racket against the fence. Fortunately it was not a refereed match or I would have been docked a point. Every time I looked at the fat guy, I knew he knew I was the better player but that if he just let me beat myself, he could win. What was worse, I began to worry how I would explain my loss to you guys."

Billy insisted, "We were all behind you. You came back and held even with him early in set three. But then..."

Billy was right. Early in the third set, the wind slowed down, and I held my serve. My corpulent opponent also won his serve because I returned the ball too hard and over the base line. "Fatso" had served first, so he led by one game with six games being set and match.

"You remember it was my turn to serve at five games to four," I said. "I just tried to keep calm. Chubby took his time toweling-off before waddling into position. He knew the longer he took to return to the service line, the more irritated I would get. He was baiting me."

"So that's why you were bouncing the ball faster and faster on the cement," Billy said. "I got worried when I saw you taking out your frustration on the ball. Then you blasted in that first serve. I thought you had *aced* him. We all cheered. The ball definitely hit right on the service line."

"I thought I taught him a lesson," I said. "When he called the ball out, I could not believe it. You remember I went back to the service line and hit a faster second serve that fell long of the service box. Suddenly I was three points down. After that, I blew my last forehand over the baseline. It was clearly out, and I lost the match."

"I couldn't believe you lost to that loser," Billy said. "He wouldn't have been able to hit the ball with power if his life depended on it."

"I lost to a guy who didn't even play *real* tennis. I just fell into my chair and threw my racket in my bag. My shirt was dripping with sweat, I felt glued to my chair, and I didn't want to get up and shake his hand. He had not won. I lost."

What Billy didn't know was when I went to the net for the traditional handshake, I could still hear my mother's words repeating inside my head: "Pride cometh before a fall."

It was getting dark outside Paul's. We both needed to get home and do our schoolwork, so we paid separate checks and left. As we walked out the door into the brisk night, Billy reached for his car keys. The lot was dark as the only street lamp was out. He pulled-up the zipper to his letter jacket to shut out the late March cold. As I was about to get into my car, he said, "Forget it. This season will definitely be better."

"I hope so," I replied. As I closed the car door, Mom's words still echoed in my head.

6
ELLIOTT

ONE EARLY SEPTEMBER AFTERNOON, TIM and Elliott were sitting at Little Mauricio's restaurant finishing their Italian subs. "How did you get today off?" Elliott, the older of the two, asked.

"Teacher work day. And you?"

Elliott, who wore jeans and a Busch Gardens-issued security shirt, replied, "I'm always off on Fridays. New boss at Busch. Do you like my shirt? It's a real chick magnet."

Tim knew from another student's father who worked at Busch, the company did not allow its employees to wear any part of the uniform unless on the way to or from work, but he let it drop. He did not want to challenge his friend. Instead, he said, "So any news on what four-year college you'll attend? Or have you decided on the Marine Corps? I know you applied to both, and you finish your two-year program at Thomas Nelson this December."

Elliott sat back. "Yeah, I applied to Mary Washington but still haven't decided if it's college or the Marine Corps."

Just then the thirty-something buxom waitress with blonde hair, bright red lipstick, and an Eastern European accent asked them if they wanted dessert. Both said "No, just the check, please." Elliott followed up with, "Where are you from?"

"Belarus," she answered. "Do you know where that is?"

Elliott stumbled on the question and Tim whispered to him, "Near Russia."

"Near Russia," Elliott said.

"Good for you," she replied. "At least someone knows where my country is located."

As she walked off slowly, she made a point of undulating her hips to show off her posterior. Looking over her shoulder, she said in a husky but sensual voice, "I'll be right back. Don't go anywhere."

Elliott was immediately smitten. "I would sure like to take her back to my place sometime when my Dad's not home, or we could go to her place. I think I'll make my move when she returns."

Tim smiled nervously, remembering when he and Elliott had first met. Two years ago when Elliott was a graduating senior and Tim was a sophomore, Elliott had approached Tim and said, "You're new here. Where you from?" When Tim replied that he had transferred in from an overseas school, Elliott, who had previously gone to high school in upstate New York, immediately understood Tim's bewilderment at finding himself in rural Virginia.

Elliott had known that Tim was going through what he had experienced the year before, the comments of,

"You're not from around here, are you?" or the tight smiles accompanied by, "Well, bless your heart, isn't that awfully far away?" Because of that, Elliott told Tim, "We outsiders have to stick together. We can watch each other's back." Though they weren't in many classes together, Elliott had the same lunch period, and Tim never had to sit alone. If Elliott went to a party, he dragged Tim along. Two summers ago, when Elliott graduated, Tim wiped away some tears as he watched Elliott walk across the stage. Elliott had put Tim on the guest list as a family member. The only real family he had was his dad, Peter.

As the waitress returned with the check, Elliott pushed his Busch Gardens-issued .38 revolver further under his jacket and winked at Tim. Tim knew Elliott was supposed to leave it at work or at home, but he had to admit it gave Elliott a certain gravitas. Elliott had told him he had spent hours on the practice range and invited Tim to learn, but Tim had never been up for it. As he sat there, Tim thought, *Elliott's ready for anything.*

The waitress put the check on the table, and Elliott picked it up, pulled out his credit card, and gave it to her. "That's for both of us," he said. When Tim offered to pay, Elliott replied, "I'm working and you're still in school. Let me get this." The voluptuous blonde left but quickly returned with the receipt. She gave each of them a card with her name so they could rate the restaurant and service.

Elliott was about to ask her out when she asked Tim for the card she had given him She wrote her cell phone number on the back and handed it to him. She then said in a deep, arousing voice, "Keep that. Call me and you can rate my service in person." Tim turned red. No girl had ever given him her phone number, and this was a sexy older woman. He wondered why she had not chosen his older companion. True, Elliott who was slightly overweight, appeared to be a bit sedentary, but he was wearing the "chick magnet," and he projected the self-confidence that Tim longed for.

As they were leaving, Tim showed Elliott the phone number and commented that he did not plan to call. Elliott quickly responded, "Don't look a gift horse in the mouth. She obviously likes you, dude. Give her a call. She's probably turned-on by your green eyes and blond hair. Go for it."

Lack of experience with women caused Tim to rely on his friend for advice. But this time he was too afraid to take it. He looked at Elliott. "Do you remember the day we went kayaking? It was the summer after your graduation."

Elliott said, "Yeah. What's that gotta do with the blonde?"

The summer of Tim's junior year, they had gone kayaking together at a local river. Elliott, who was an experienced kayaker, had chosen the river to avoid rapids or rough water. He taught Tim the principles and they set out. Tim was doing well until he caught a paddle on a branch, overturned his kayak, and ended up in the water. Tim did not know how to flip the kayak. He was a strong swimmer but the kayak held him down. Elliott dove in the water, pulled him out from under the kayak, and dragged him onto a small island. He then jumped back in the water and retrieved the kayaks before they had floated too far down-river. Tim sat shivering on the island and waiting for him to come back.

When Elliott returned, the two sat there for a while. Seeing Tim shivering, Elliott retrieved a jacket from his kayak. "Take this," he said. "It happens to all of us. Don't feel bad, but you sure looked funny, sort of like a drowned rat." Tim already knew he could count on his friend to have his back, but this was just one more time that Elliott had come through for him.

As they sat there on the small island, Elliott said, "I never told you why I came to live with my dad in Virginia." He looked at his feet, not making eye contact, and seemed to be pondering what to say.

"You don't have to if you don't want to. It's not my business."

But Elliott answered, "I want to. It's just, it's just… hard. You know I lived with my mom and my stepdad in New York, near Albany, and went to high school there. One day, sophomore year, I came home on the bus." He stopped for a moment and took a deep breath. "When I opened the door, I saw the two of them lying there on the floor. They weren't moving. Then I saw the blood on my mom's shirt. I looked at my stepdad, and he had a hole in the side of his head and his hand was still clutching the gun. I wanted to scream, but no sound came out of my mouth. I just sank to my knees. I don't know how long it was before I dialed 911. The authorities called my real dad and shortly after, I came to live with him here in Virginia." Elliott's eyes glazed over as he spoke and turned vacant. It was the first and last time they discussed the incident. Tim knew it was rare for Elliott to open up to anyone, and he was happy that Elliott had trusted him.

Awakening from his momentary reverie about their

kayaking adventure, Tim said, "I thought you wanted to date her, Elliott. You should ask her out. You've always come through for me. I know if it were you, you'd call her, but I can't. You have it all together. You have a full-time job, you're a college student, and have a girlfriend, and the Marines want you. You and Karen have been together since high school. I don't even have a girlfriend."

Elliott laughed and said, "As for Karen, you know that Supertramp line that goes, 'Take a look at my girlfriend, she's the only one I got.' You know what follows?"

"Yeah," Tim replied. "I remember the words. 'Not much of a girlfriend, I never seem to get a lot.'"

Tim had been at Elliott's house playing Magic, a fantasy card game, a few weeks before their lunch at Little Mauricio's. When they first began to play earlier in the year, Elliott explained to his girlfriend that Magic is a game where wizards battled one another using spells and artifacts found on the cards, which were traded between players. Karen was not interested. That night was no different. The tall, quiet girl watched but refused to participate. Tim was surprised when Karen spoke up and mentioned something about her and Elliott moving in together. Elliott cut her off by curtly remarking, "We've discussed this before. You know I can't do that now, Karen. I'm waiting for my college application to be accepted or for the Marines to take me. Once I decide between the two, I'm gone. But we can always see each other one weekend a month if I go to school or Skype if the marines send me far away." He pushed his chair back and stood. "Tim and I have got to go buy more cards. I know you don't want to come, so you can either wait here or I'll swing by your house after." Tim said nothing. Karen chose to go home.

But they had not gone to get Magic cards. Elliott just wanted to have a beer alone with his friend, and they ended up at the Ale House. Tim being only sixteen, Elliott wanted to order two beers and then give one to him. Tim quickly said, "I'll have a diet Coke." They sat in silence and listened to music until Tim had to go home. Before he left, Elliott told him, "You know Tim, you're my bud. Friends forever."

Before their lunch at Little Mauricio's in the fall of his junior year, Tim had not seen as much of his friend as in the past. Tim was busy playing first singles for the high school tennis team and trying to improve his grade point average for college. Elliott attended community college, took online courses, and worked at Busch Gardens. Though the two did not get together as often as when Elliott was in high school or during that summer, Elliott remained a vital part of Tim's life. On Saturday nights, and whenever Tim was not studying or on the tennis court, they continued to play Magic. Their games ran late into the night. Elliott was always a fierce competitor and would smile when he bested Tim at the game, but it was a good-natured smile with more camaraderie than egotism.

At the end of their lunch at Little Mauricio's, Elliott invited Tim for Thanksgiving dinner with him and his dad. Although Tim told him he had to eat with his family, Elliott made him promise to stop over after he had dinner at home. Tim, anxious to see if Elliott chose the marines or Mary Washington, said he would be there.

Elliott's dad, Peter, prepared a sumptuous Thanksgiving dinner, and Tim was sorry he had eaten at home before going. A balding, jovial sixty-year-old with a well-trimmed beard, Peter was the cafeteria supervisor at Winstead Academy, a local private school. Tim had never seen him without a smile on his face. After the meal, Elliott announced that both Mary Washington and the Marines had accepted him. He had not decided yet but expected that he would make his choice soon. After Elliott made his announcement, Peter was ecstatic. He beamed with joy. Things looked like they would finally come together for his son.

Late December was busy for everyone. Tim took his SATs and began preparing for a family Christmas with his grandmother in Rockaway, New Jersey. Wednesday night, three days before Christmas, he got a frantic call from Peter asking if Elliott was with him. At first, Tim did not recognize Peter's shaky voice when he asked, "Is that you, Tim?" Without waiting for an answer, Peter continued, "Elliott and I argued. I only wanted to help him. I wanted to see his acceptance to Mary Washington so I could help him financially. I didn't mean to… I didn't mean to upset him. When I went upstairs to talk to him, I found a letter for me on his bed. Elliott's gone. His gun is missing from the closet where he keeps it, but his car's still in the driveway. I thought he might be with you."

Tim told his mom and dad that Elliott and his dad had a fight, Elliott was gone, and Peter was worried. Not wanting to upset his parents further, he did not tell them that Elliott's gun was missing and this was much more serious than a father-son argument. He only explained that Peter had asked him if he knew where Elliott might be and said he had promised to check out some of Elliott's normal hang-outs. Tim's dad, seeing his worried expression, asked twice if he wanted company in his search, but Tim did not want to concern his father, so he said, "Thanks, but I can handle this on my own."

* * *

He drove straight to Peter's condominium, and the two of them spent hours looking for Elliott at all his known haunts. They continued in the dark, driving around the extended neighborhood, each time stopping and calling Elliott's name. When they returned to the condominium around ten, Elliott's car was still in the driveway. Tim had been trying Elliott's cell for hours, but it kept going directly to voice mail. He was exhausted but did not want to leave Peter. Finally, the older man told him to go home and said he now planned to contact the police. He promised to call Tim with any news.

Tim had never seen Peter like this. His jovial manner had disappeared, and his shoulders hunched under the weight of worry. During the unsuccessful odyssey to find Elliott, Peter looked broken and appeared to get older by the minute. Tim did not want to ask what was in the letter, so he focused on finding his friend. Tim's nerves were frazzled, as he knew he had to leave for New Jersey early the next morning.

When Tim returned home, his parents were still up. "Did you find Elliott?" they asked. Tim shook his head. Seeing that Tim was exhausted, his mom counseled, "Don't worry, things will turn out just fine. Get some rest. Elliott will probably return in the morning and make up with his dad."

Tim fretted long into the night, wondering if he should have told his parents how serious this was and waiting for Peter to call. He finally fell asleep on a downstairs couch.

Peter called early the next morning as Tim and his family were preparing to leave. Tim was putting his suitcase in the car when he got the call.

In a quivering voice, Peter said, "The police found Elliott's body this morning. There was a self-inflicted bullet hole in the side of his head. They said his body was slumped on the grass next to the Colonial Parkway. I had to go and identify the body. I've just returned home and wanted you to know. I've got to make arrangements for the funeral, probably after Christmas. I'll let you know."

Tim grabbed the car door to keep from falling. In doing so, he dropped his cell phone on the gravel driveway. His head was spinning, and he felt nauseous. His parents, who had just locked the house and were approaching the car, rushed to his aid. They knew he had been out the previous night looking for his friend.

Tim's dad asked, "What happened?"

Tim gasped, "Elliott's dead. He's really dead! Why, why, oh why?"

"Is there something we can do?" his dad asked softly. "Is Peter okay?"

"There's nothing," Tim said. "Nothing at all. Elliott's gone. He shot himself in the head with his own gun. The stupid bastard. Why the fuck did he do it? Why did he want to leave? Why couldn't he trust me? I'm his friend, for Christ's sake!"

"I meant for Peter?" his dad responded quietly.

"No! The funeral has been delayed until after Christmas.

We might as well go to New Jersey. Peter promised to call later."

Tim's mom and dad reached out and held him. They could only try to comfort him. Elliott had been to the house many times and their pain, although not as acute as Tim's, made them feel impotent. They reached out in prayer for support, but Tim turned away. He was not ready to listen.

Tim's motions were robotic as he got into the car for the drive to Grandma's house. He put on his headphones and shut out the world. They had to stop shortly after they began. Tim jumped out of the car and puked on the side of the road. When they arrived in New Jersey, Tim's grandmother was overjoyed to see him, but she had been forewarned. Tim's dad had called her while at a rest stop and given her the news. She tried to comfort him but to no avail. For the next few days and even after their return to Williamsburg, Elliott's death overshadowed all. Tim spent his days closeted in his headphones, reflecting on what Peter had told him.

While Tim was in New Jersey, Peter called him and recounted in detail what happened. Most of it he had told Tim before, but he had not told him what was in the letter. Peter said, "In his letter, Elliott confessed that he had lied to me about being accepted to Mary Washington and the Marine Corps. In fact, he had not even applied. He said he was sorry and ashamed for lying and felt worthless, that he had let me down and life was not worth living. He wanted to see his mom again."

At the funeral, Tim counted few attendees: Peter, Elliott's half-brother, who flew in from San Francisco,

Elliott's girlfriend Karen, Tim's parents, and a few others from Elliott's church. Tim was in a daze and thought, *If I had only called Elliott more often. If Elliott had only come to me. I was his best friend. Why didn't he tell me what was going on?*

Tim blamed himself, Peter blamed himself, and even the girlfriend blamed herself. Elliott's pastor tried to explain it all away, but the few attendees felt empty and lost. Elliott was never a popular person at school, at work or even at church, but he was always a good friend to those who knew him well. Tim could not think about it for a long time, and he stopped going to church.

Peter later told Tim that Elliott wanted him to have all his Magic cards. Elliott had left Peter his car. He left nothing to the girlfriend. Tim began to spend his free time, the time he and Elliott had used to play Magic, with Peter. They spoke about many things, but for a long while, Elliott was not one of them.

7
TOO GOOD TO BE TRUE

"I'LL CALL MY DAD RIGHT now," Christy said. The short, athletic, blue-eyed blonde pushed back her shoulder-length hair from her ears and pulled her cell phone from her shoulder bag. She hit contacts, then her dad's number, and put the phone to her ear. Christy aborted the call when Tim, her tall, sandy-haired boyfriend, said, "Don't do that. I've always gotten by on my own. I don't need any help." Tim was busy checking Amtrak 95's arrival time on his smart phone.

"We've got a few minutes," he said. "Let's stay under the platform roof until your train comes. The sky is beginning to turn darker." Tim pulled Christy's heavy suitcase under the covered area running along the platform. Flower baskets full of blooming red, white, and blue petunias still adorned the white station columns. The town of Williamsburg had placed them there for the Fourth of July. Until the previous

Monday, Christy had expected Tim's travel bags to be alongside hers.

The two Lafayette high school graduates met the previous year during tennis season. Tim, who had always admired Christy from afar, was surprised when she plopped down next to him on the school bus that was taking both the boys and girls teams to play against Hampton Roads Academy. That was the first match of the year but not the last time the two sat together. By then, Tim ranked number one for the Lafayette Rams boys' team and Christy number five for the girls. Christy was not as focused on tennis as Tim, but she was a natural athlete and excelled at most sports she attempted.

Since winter of his senior year, when Elliott, his best friend, committed suicide, Tim had thrown himself into tennis with a fierce passion and a desire to block out all else. He worked hard on his East coast tennis ranking so he could get a tennis scholarship and tried to keep his grade point average at a "B". Christy, an all-around "A" student, always dreamed of attending the University of Pennsylvania. The school had an excellent biochemistry program and offered a great summer internship before college began in the fall. Christy's dad had attended the school, and with her grades, it had been all too simple for her to get in. She looked forward to college and then working in the chemical industry.

After Elliott's death, Tim had been lost. Elliott had been like an older brother. Tim, dazzled by Christy's looks and her personality, was captivated by the attention she showered on him. They soon became more than friends. He never had a friend who was a girl, not to mention a girlfriend. Several months previous, the two had decided to take the plunge. It was the first time for both of them but they managed to succeed at what came naturally. After the first time, they felt less awkward and began to meld as one. Tim still had enough of his religious training to believe that he should stay with one and only one partner. However, he no longer attended church and was far away enough away from the gospel to feel comfortable about not waiting for marriage. They had decided they wanted to stay together, and Tim applied to U Penn as well. The university accepted him even though his grades were weaker than Christy's. They even offered him a $30,000 tennis scholarship. The coach also promised he could work at the campus' indoor tennis center to make extra money for his room and board. It was perfect.

The summer after Christy and Tim graduated, they spent days with each other, Tim teaching tennis at the local tennis and swim club where Christy worked as a lifeguard. Not only were they inseparable, they loved the same movies, the same old doo-wop and country music groups, and the same sports. Tim was not the swimmer Christy was, but they both liked kayaking on the creeks that led to the York River. When they were not working, they took Christy's dad's kayak to a creek near Tim's home.

They planned almost everything together. They assumed that they would live together in an apartment somewhere in downtown Philly just off campus. Christy's dad had already been looking online for them, and Christy knew just what she wanted. Something small but within walking distance of her classes. Tim would work at the tennis center and Christy had her internship. It was set. By mid-July, they had their train tickets and prepared to depart mid-August for Philadelphia.

Tim called Christy on the Monday before they were to leave for Philly. His voice was weak and raspy. "The scholarship is off," he said. "The coach was apologetic but budget cuts have eliminated all tennis scholarships except for their top three choices. I am number five on the list."

Loans were out of the question. Tim did not want to spend his life repaying the government what he had borrowed. His honesty kept him from even considering taking the loan and then defaulting on payment. He heard of others who had taken years and most of their post-college income to pay off the loans and still others who had never repaid their loan. How would he and Christy live together after college? Tim wanted to coach tennis for a while after he graduated college, then maybe teach history in a high school somewhere near where Christy found a job. Christy hoped to find a job somewhere on the East coast, maybe Virginia, North Carolina, or Pennsylvania. Her father had mentioned Dow Chemical in North Carolina.

As they stood on the platform, Christy had to try one more time. "I know you said 'no'," Christy pleaded. "But let me call my dad. I'm sure he can help."

Christy's dad was a well-known architect and had recently given $100,000 to the University of Pennsylvania to help pay for a new auditorium. A graduate of the university, where he had played varsity football, he had contributed substantial sums over previous years. The recent donation and previous ones gave him some leverage with certain administrators and a certain pull at U Penn. Christy's eyes turned a deeper blue as she focused intensely on Tim, waiting for his answer. She thought Tim seemed smaller somehow without his tennis letter jacket. He looked at the ground.

"I guess we didn't plan on this happening," he said.

"Please, Tim," Christy whispered.

"Okay," he said. "If your dad can fix this, it will save me from attending Tidewater Community college this fall."

Christy knew her dad was leaving on a flight from Richmond to LaGuardia Airport in Queens. He was going to a meeting at Trump Tower across from Central Park in Manhattan; something about a new property that the family wanted to acquire. Christy quickly dialed her dad's number. The phone rang once, twice, three times, and then went to voice mail. Her father's message came on. "Leave your name at the sound of the beep." Tim helped Christy put her bags on the Amtrak business class car. Then he slowly stepped off the train.

As train 95 to Philadelphia pulled out of the station, it began to rain. The sky was much darker, and the air had turned colder.

8

THE LONG WAY HOME

IT WAS RAINING HARD ON the Sunday Tim told his parents he was going to accompany them to church. To say that they were surprised would be an understatement. They knew the reason he had not set foot in the church for the last year and a half, and they had given him some space. The last Sunday service he attended was in his junior year, just before Christmas. That was the year his best friend, Elliott, shot himself in the head two days before Christmas Eve. It was now the summer after graduation, and Tim was still looking for a college to attend.

Tim had never been able to talk about Elliott's death. He blamed himself and continued to run the events through his mind. "If I had only called Elliott more often or if I had seen that Elliott was not himself, somehow not right." Elliott's pastor had tried to explain it all away at the funeral, but it still made no sense to Tim. He wondered how God could have allowed such a thing to happen.

Tim's family were no strangers to what people might call miracles. They called these God's blessings, God's grace or God's law of good. Tim's grandmother had fallen out of a second-story window when she was only a few months old. The doctors said she would never be normal and might even die. The church prayed, and she not only recovered but was still going strong at the age of ninety-two. Tim's granduncle had been burned almost beyond recognition in a chemical fire. He had burns over ninety percent of his body. The church and the family prayed again. He too was healed. Tim saw him years later, and he had only some small scars on his face and body. Many years earlier during World War II, the same uncle, an Air Force pilot, made it back to his base in the Pacific, flying his bullet-ridden B-59 bomber with only one working engine. The working engine mysteriously died just as they touched down. Tim respected family history but could never understand why God let his grandmother and granduncle live and not Elliott. Perhaps there was no church praying for Elliott, maybe no one had cared enough to pray, or maybe God just didn't care.

Tim's parents were teaching Sunday school so Tim walked into the church auditorium alone. When he looked to the right, he saw Miss de Longe sitting in her usual seat in the next- to-last pew. She always sat by the window so she could look out over what she called "God's beautiful world." Although Tim had not been to church for a while, his parents had kept him up to date on the old lady who had always showed him so much affection and who had been his Sunday school teacher. Six months previously,

Miss de Longe, who was about eighty-five, had broken her hip in a fall. The doctors said she was too old and the hip would never heal right. She would never walk again. She was absent from church for two months. After that, her son brought her in a wheel chair. Several months later, she dropped the wheelchair and used a walker. Then one day about a month ago, she walked in on her own power, praising God and taking her usual seat by the window.

Tim slid over and sat next to Miss de Longe. He knew she originally came from Louisiana and was born to a landholding family of the old South who had built the first library in her part of the state. Though she seemed smaller and frailer, he could tell her spirit was still invincible. People said she had what the Bible called the "spirit of God" in her.

Miss de Longe touched Tim's arm and then gave it a squeeze. "It's nice to see you, Tim," she said. "I've kept you in my prayers." Her piercing violet eyes reminded Tim of the expression, "The eyes are the windows of the soul." As she looked out the window, she had the most beautiful smile. Turning back to Tim, she said, "If you'll drive my car, I'd like to take you for coffee and brunch today at the Art Café. You know where it is, Dear. It's just down the road. Just let your folks know you'll be with me."

After church, Tim talked to his parents and then drove off with Miss de Longe. Once seated in the café, the two ordered coffee and crumb cakes and settled back in the comfortable chairs. The café was a mixture of eclectic furniture, which Tim thought he would not have put together. The wooden benches, flowered deep-seated sofas, writing tables, and high circular tables with stool-like chairs all somehow worked as a whole. The exotic blue-design Mexican tiles around the bar gave the place a bohemian ambiance.

Miss de Longe patted Tim on the arm. "So tell me what you have been up to over the last year and a half. I heard a lot from your parents, but it's not the same as getting it from the horse's mouth."

Tim told her about his tennis, his girlfriend Christy, and their thwarted plans to go to the University of Pennsylvania together, but failed to mention that they also planned to live together. He did tell her things had recently begun to fall apart, and he might have to go to a local junior college and live at home while Christy went to school in Philadelphia. He never mentioned Elliott's death, but he knew that she knew it was on his mind. His parents and Miss de Longe were good friends, and he was certain they had told her why he left the church.

"Tim," she said, "Your friend Elliott's death was a tragedy, but it was never your fault the same way it was never God's fault. Sometimes, we are too focused on what we want and what we need to do, and then we trip and fall. Sometimes we fall badly, and we think we can't ever be forgiven or whole again. But God loves us like a mother, and when we open our hearts to Him, he shows us the path. I'd like to think your friend Elliott understands that now."

She stopped for a moment and then continued, "It took me a while to figure it out. When I fell and broke my hip, I was so full of my own pride about how I wanted to be independent and how my faith in God would heal me. It took weeks, but I learned how to get out of myself and into

God. I found that it was God's spirit in me, God's strength in me, and God's love in me, which gave me the power to walk again. It's like the man said, 'I can of my own self do nothing.'"

Tim stared intently at the elderly woman, waiting for her to continue. She was quiet for a moment and allowed Tim to process what she had been telling him. "Do you remember when I was your Sunday school teacher? You used to love the Bible stories and their meaning for our lives. Remember the story of Peter, who sees Jesus walking on the water? Peter tries to walk on the water but gets afraid and begins to drown. Jesus reaches out his hand and holds him up. Christ always will hold us up if we are willing to reach out our hand. That's why Jesus told the parable about the prodigal son. The boy leaves, goes on a long journey, and spends all his inheritance trying to find happiness only to realize he has nothing. When he returns, his father gives him the best robe and a ring and still calls him his son. We think, in our pride, that we can walk away from God. We can leave the church, we can stop reading the Bible, and we can pretend we don't care because the world doesn't care. But God is the father in Jesus' parable, and He is always waiting for our return. He expects us to come back and claim our inheritance, our true self."

Tim quietly listened to the grandmotherly woman who was leading him toward something different. She had explained that he did not have to earn God's love; it was freely given. If that were true, maybe there was a way forward? Maybe God could help him get into the University of Pennsylvania and be with Christy. Tim slowly began to see that it went further than just getting into college, being ranked in tennis on the East coast, or even being with Christy. It was about spending his life with God. Suddenly, he remembered the words to an old hymn he had sung at church. "I once was lost but now I'm found, was blind but now I see."

Miss de Longe took out her purse to pay for the lunch. "You know, Tim," she said, "we need to do this more often. I didn't realize how much I missed having you around. Just remember dear, you are loved."

About a month after Christy left for Philadelphia, Tim was at the Williamsburg train station with a new ticket in his pocket. Christy's dad had some connections at Drexel University in Philadelphia. He had obtained an interview for Tim where he would discuss a possible tennis scholarship. Tim was going to speak with the tennis coach and admissions people. Drexel was collocated with parts of U Penn. Christy, who had gone early to spend the summer there, was going to host him for the weekend. He looked forward to seeing Christy, whom he missed with the passion of a young man experiencing his first and perhaps only true love. But there was some uneasiness in his mind as he ruminated about their relationship. "Christy and I are going to have to talk. That is what happens when you turn your life over to God. He becomes part of everything you do and everything you are. And you need to live in accordance with His rules." Tim didn't know what the interviews would bring, but this time it was not just about him. He was going to take Miss de Longe's advice and live beyond himself.

For a moment, he thought he saw Miss de Longe waving at him from the far end of the platform. When he looked again, there was no one, and he realized he must have been mistaken. As the train pulled out, the words of a song drifted through his mind.

When I was young, it seemed that life was so wonderful, a miracle. Won't you tell me what I've learned and who I am?

Tim realized the words were from the Supertramp song "Logical" that had been one of Elliott's favorites. Tim wanted to believe Elliott had learned who he was. The sunrays seemed to glisten and dance on everything: the trees, the train windows, the seats and the passengers. The weather report predicted showers for the afternoon, but for now, the sunlight was enough.

9

SOMETHING THAT COUNTS

GRAD SCHOOL NOW FINISHED FOR the spring semester, Tim left hot and muggy D.C. behind for what he hoped would be a cooler Chicago summer. When his seatmate on the plane informed him that Chicago was having a heat wave, Tim was glad he had decided to wear his summer suit. In fact, it was the only summer suit he owned, an olive green drip-dry. His research assistantship at American University allowed him to attend the university and pay for lodging but he had little extra money. He had paid for this Chicago trip out of his own pocket, and his ticket had put a deep hole in his savings.

Several months earlier, Tim discovered that his church was starting a center in Southwest Chicago. The church planned to offer Sunday school on weekday mornings and English and math tutoring in the afternoons. All the other volunteers were from a private college located near

St. Louis. Lodging and food would be free, but the job itself was gratis. Tim didn't care. He told his Washington friends, "This is my chance to do something that counts."

Mrs. Johnson met Tim at the arrivals section of O'Hare airport and escorted him to her new Jeep. Annie Johnson was in her forties, had striking blonde hair and an athletic build which was the result of swimming and playing a lot of tennis. Her husband, Mike, was a wealthy Chicago businessman who belonged to Tim's church. Mike had agreed to support the center financially by housing and feeding some of the volunteers and providing a white van for transportation. After they left O'Hare, Mrs. Johnson took a circuitous route around Chicago. After about forty minutes, they arrived at a two-room storefront building on 71st street between South Emerald Avenue and Halstead.

The center, a small, white brick building, had a black and white sign over the door which read, "Christian Center, All Welcome." The building's windows had grates and the door had a padlock, which was closed at night. An old mat on a stone slab allowed visitors to clean their feet before entering, and a torn green awning protected the entrance from the summer rain.

Young staff members Mark, Karen, Kathy, and Bill greeted Tim and Mrs. Johnson as they entered. By the manner in which way they interacted and smiled at each other, it was obvious that Kathy and Bill were a couple. Red haired, green-eyed Karen immediately attracted Tim's attention. She wore a small diamond engagement ring and later told Tim that her boyfriend would pick her up at the end of the month and drive her back to Saint Louis. Tall and skinny, Mark appeared to be a loner. His long brown hair fell down over his forehead and almost covered his glasses, and his beard was not well trimmed.

During lunch, which the staff served to themselves and the kids, Mark took out his wallet and showed Tim a photo of his girlfriend. The girl in the picture was dressed like a hippie with multicolored pants and a yellow sun hat that partially hid her long brown hair. After lunch, Karen showed Tim where he could store his suitcase until the end of the day. Tim's impression of her continued to be positive. *A sweet, attractive, and friendly girl*, he thought.

Tim removed his jacket and tie and rolled up the sleeves of his worn white shirt so he could get to work. The staff introduced him to some of the African American kids who came to morning Sunday school, lunch, and stayed for math and English in the afternoon. One small kid, Stan, stood out from the rest. About six years old, he had dark sparkling eyes, short brown kinky hair, walnut skin, and a winning smile. Stan was dressed in raggedy white sneakers, ripped tan shorts, and a timeworn white shirt that looked like his mother had recently ironed it. "Stan the man," as he was called, could not read but he learned things from TV and the streets around him.

That evening, the center closed at the habitual time, five p.m. The volunteers piled into the Johnson's old white van, and Mark drove the group back to Wilmette just north of Chicago. Driving out of the neighborhood, Tim could see they were leaving behind the old, wooden house neighborhood to pick up a circular highway. A view of the Chicago skyscape loomed in the distance. Avoiding the center of the city, they arrived in Evanston, and Tim got a good view of the white domed, ornate, almost

Hindu-looking Bahai Temple with its luxurious gardens surrounded by water on three sides. They drove past the Wilmette Boat Club and basin where the sailing vessels dotted the harbor like seagulls floating on the water. After dropping off the two girls at another Wilmette home, the van pulled into a circular drive off Sheridan Road. Tim gasped in surprise when he saw Lake Michigan just across the yard.

The Johnson's house, a mansion the likes of which Tim had only seen on TV, had a terrific view of the water and a large outdoor swimming pool situated between the house and the lake. Tim, Bill, and Mark ate a dinner of hamburgers and green beans prepared by Mrs. Johnson, played some Ping-Pong in the recreation room, and then retired to a large bedroom where three beds had been set up for them.

Tim was so tired he forgot to use the acne pads he had brought with him and tumbled into bed. He regretted it the next morning when he looked in the mirror. His face was a battlefield full of exploding bunkers and jagged foxholes. In high school, they called him pizza face. College friends were kinder. Tim tried many remedies, but the acne never went away, and he was extremely self-conscious. Looking in the mirror had become a daily torture.

Breakfast was at six-thirty. Mrs. Johnson had prepared bacon, scrambled eggs, and toast. Once done, the group jumped in the white van, picked up the girls, and left for southwest Chicago. It took over an hour to drive around the city to avoid downtown traffic. Tim soon realized that they had begun their drive in heaven and ended in hell. In the morning light, 71st Street was a wasteland of boarded-up buildings, empty lots, and crack houses. The wind pushed garbage, gritty soil, and dust from decrepit buildings back and forth like an out-of-control street sweeper. The houses seemed to be disintegrating right in front of Tim's eyes. Vacant lots dotted the neighborhood. Along Halstead Avenue, the only commercial establishments were Callahan's market and Harrison's funeral home. On South Emerald, many of the homes still standing were boarded up. Former owners had nailed wooden planks across the windows and put grates in front of the broken glass on splintering doors. Tim remembered that the Johnsons had mentioned at breakfast, "Chicago is always windy, and in the summer, downtown can be pretty hot and dirty." But, for Tim, this went beyond hot and dirty.

At nine o'clock when the van arrived, fifteen neighborhood kids were already lined up in front. They appeared to have been there for some time. Tim later discovered that most of them lived on 71st, Emerald, or Halstead. Kids in that neighborhood did not walk beyond a radius of five blocks. It was too dangerous to stray.

The kids had not had breakfast, so that was the first order of the day. Then there were Bible classes in the morning where the small kids colored in Bible story coloring books. The older kids learned Bible stories along with how to apply Christian principles in daily life. It was simple stuff like not fighting with your siblings, seeing other people as God's children, and not judging people by how they looked.

Tim had the youngest group. There were only two kids, "Stan the man" and a little girl named Mary. The girl had pigtails with pink ribbons tied around them and a pink dress that appeared to be ragged but clean. When Tim told them, "God is love," Stan surprised Tim. "What do you mean?" he said. "My dad left us. My grandma died. My dog Willy got run over and died. What do you mean God is love!"

Stan's father had taught him two things: how to shake hands and look people in the eyes. When Stan turned five, his father left to find a job in another state and there had been no news from him for about a year. Stan's grandmother passed away a little after his Dad left. His mother had three kids to care for on her own. About a month before Tim arrived, a car killed Willy, the dog Stan's mother got from the ASPCA. One Saturday night, Stan forgot to close the back door and Willy got out of the house and onto the street. Stan told Tim, "Momma says it ain't good to be on the street at night, especially on Fridays and Saturdays." Tim replied, "Your momma must love you very much, and God must too, if he gave you such a nice momma." Stan just rolled his big brown eyes.

The local churches provided sandwiches and juice pouches for lunch. The free breakfast and lunch were why many of the kids came to the Bible classes. After lunch, they went over basic math and reading fundamentals. Tim began to help Stan sound out the words to a child's version of the story "Peter Pan." Tim related some of the characters in the story to superheroes Stan had seen on TV. Stan told Tim that Superman had a lot more powers than Peter Pan did. "I want to be like Superman," he said. Nevertheless, the story of "Neverland" and the "lost-boys" did strike a chord in the youngster's heart. Stan's eyes never left the pages while Tim read the story. Tim thought, *Stan is a lost boy, and I don't know if I can be his Wendy. Perhaps I'm also a lost boy.*

Tim did not realize then he really had nothing in common with Stan but their humanity. Later he would see, even with his feelings of being different and alone, he was raised in a stable home, with many opportunities and, with God's grace, a future. He was not nor ever would be a "lost boy."

Later in the afternoon, the staff and kids went for a stroll around the neighborhood. They called the stroll "the love patrol." Everywhere the kids walked, they were supposed to see God's provision. As they walked around, Tim thought, *This is going to be easier for the kids than it is for me. They don't know the way the other half lives, except what they see on TV. How can they see God's goodness in boarded-up houses, vacant lots, and crack joints?*

For about three weeks, they followed the same routine. Tim and Karen hit it off right away. Maybe it was because they looked at their faith the same way. The second Saturday, Tim invited Karen out for coffee. She accepted but reminded him in a nice way that her boyfriend, Richard, was waiting for her in St. Louis. Mark's girlfriend came up from St. Louis to spend weekends, and Kathy and Bill spent all their off hours together.

Though he never became a "Wendy," Tim's relationship with Stan grew closer as the days went by. Stan learned to read and write. He hugged Tim a lot and tagged along behind him, like the mayor of the neighborhood with his little stomach sticking out from his torn shirt. On the second Monday, Tim was at the center avoiding looking in mirrors, as he could not break his self-conscious obsession with how others viewed his acne-scarred face.

Stan interrupted his somber thoughts by hugging him and saying, "You're beautiful. I wish you were my dad." The little boy looked beyond what his eyes saw. It suddenly dawned on Tim that when Stan looked at him, he looked with his heart and gave his heart without reservation.

From that moment on, they were inseparable. Stan would be at the center door every morning waiting for Tim, and they would spend the day together with either Bible studies or English after the walk around the neighborhood.

On Tim's next-to-last Friday night as a volunteer, the group was closing the center as usual. Suddenly, a young black woman rushed in. "Have you seen Stanley?" she asked. She was dressed in a fast-food restaurant uniform with a cap that said "Roy Rogers," and she looked like she was in her mid-twenties. Her straightened black hair was styled in a short "Prince Valiant" pageboy. Her troubled dark brown eyes seemed clouded, and she looked close to tears.

Tim was at the front and asked her if she were Stan's mother. When she nodded, he said, "Nice to meet you, I've heard a lot about you. Stan left here several hours ago."

The woman, who said her name was Sarah, could barely speak, but Tim was able to get "Not home… brother was supposed to watch… kicked him out on the street."

Tim told her, "He couldn't have gone too far. He's an obedient kid, and he told me his mom told him to stay in the neighborhood."

"That's right," the young mother said. "He's not supposed to leave the yard and never even go outside the house on Friday and Saturday nights."

Tim quickly came up with a game plan. "Stan's mom

and I will search Emerald Street. Mark and Karen, you take Halstead. Bill and Kathy, you take 71st Street. We'll meet back in an hour. Make sure everyone is back here by six-thirty at the latest. It's probably not wise to be walking around after that."

Tim and Sarah began walking down 71st, looking behind abandoned buildings and crossing vacant lots. Sarah, speaking in a soft voice, told Tim that Stan was her second child. She became pregnant and married her husband, Jefferson, when she was eighteen and he was twenty-five. Jefferson, a divorced father with a nine-year-old son, decided to marry her because he needed someone to take care of his son, Leroy. It had not been easy for Sarah, married at eighteen and soon responsible for a stepson and her first child, Latisha. "It's been hard," she said. "I had Stanley when I was twenty-three. Jefferson was thirty when Stan was born, and he left me about a year ago just after he turned thirty-five. He had high ambitions and felt weighed down by a family. I've not heard from him since."

Sarah was twenty-eight when her husband left, and alone, except for her mom. She had a high school diploma and was able to get a job at a Roy Rogers fast-food restaurant in the downtown "loop" area. Sarah's mother took care of Stan and Latisha. Then she died of cancer. After her mom died, Sarah asked her stepson, Leroy, to watch the kids when they got out of school. Every morning, she left home at seven, took the "L" downtown and returned home around five in the afternoon. Leroy, now seventeen, had time to watch the kids. Sarah continued, "Leroy dropped out of high school and just hangs around the house chilling with his friends. He hasn't bothered to find a job and help with the rent."

Tim asked, "What happened today? Why didn't Stan go home?"

Sarah tearfully explained, "Stan did go home. Leroy was watching Stan and Latisha. He had been drinking beer, and Stan told him that he was going to tell me that Leroy took money out of the kitchen drawer. Leroy grabbed Stanley's arm and dragged him to the door. He pushed Stanley outside, slammed the door and locked it. When he looked outside about a half hour later, Stanley was missing. Leroy went back to drinking.

"At five forty-five, I arrived home and asked Leroy where Stan was. Leroy said he was outside playing, but Latisha told me what really happened. That's when I come running to the center. I thought Stanley might be there."

As they continued to walk, calling out Stan's name, a yellow Cadillac drove by slowly. "That's the local pimp," Sarah whispered. "He's also the local dealer. The police leave him alone. We have to find Stanley; it's not safe for him to be out, especially on a Friday night."

A dog barked at the other side of a vacant lot. Attracted by the noise, they crossed the lot and found Stan sitting on the ground with a dirty mongrel puppy in his arms. The puppy barked playfully and seemed pleased to have a companion. He was licking Stan's face. As they approached, Stan said, "Look what I found, momma. He's going to be my pup now that Willy died."

Sarah's voice trembled with anger. "Stanley, I told you to never leave the house except to go to the center!" Tim put his hand softly on her arm to calm her down. Tears filled her eyes, and she ran toward the little boy and swept him up in her arms. Tim grabbed the mongrel puppy who had jumped on to the ground.

"Promise me you'll never do this again," she said. Her body was shaking, and Tim wasn't sure if it was from anger, exhaustion, frustration or just plain fear of a potential disaster that had been averted.

"But Leroy…" Stan began.

"I'll deal with Leroy," she said. "Let's go home."

By the time they got back to the center, an hour had passed. The other four volunteers had given up and were waiting for Tim. When they saw Sarah and Stan, everyone started yelling, "Thank God."

Sarah touched Tim's arm. "Thank you."

Stan put his arms around Tim and, showing a full set of teeth, said, "You're my best friend."

Sarah took Stan and the puppy home. Tim wondered what she would say to Leroy. The situation did not look promising, but Tim immediately rejected the idea of going with her. It might only make matters worse. He joined the other volunteers, got in the van, and started the long trip back to Wilmette. The day had been eventful, but Stan had been found.

The next week passed too quickly. Four weeks had come and gone. It was Tim's last Friday at the center. He planned to fly back to D.C. the next morning. Stan would not leave Tim's side the whole day. When the group got into the van on Friday evening, Stan yelled at Tim, "I hate you. You're just like my dad." Tim saw tears in the little boy's eyes. Nevertheless, he noticed that Stan waved wildly as the vehicle pulled out. Looking out the van's back window, Tim saw the little boy drop his head and shoulders, turn, and slowly walk away.

During the van ride back to Wilmette and later on the plane ride to D.C., Tim wondered if it had been worth it, to give a little boy hope and then pull it away. Tim knew he had to continue trying and thought that he would probably volunteer to work at a similar center opening in Anacostia near Washington, D.C.

A few months later, Tim started working at the Anacostia center. The neighborhood was not so different from southwest Chicago. It was just hotter and muggier. Tim also began working part-time as a permanent substitute teacher in a local high school in Anacostia. When the school board refused to replace the teachers who had left, Tim, thinking of Stan, fought for permanent certified teachers for his kids. After six months, he won his fight. Tim never saw Stan again and never went back to Chicago. He continued to wonder if it all had been worth it. One thing he knew: he was not the same.

10
THE LOOK IN HIS EYES

THE SETTING SUN'S DYING RAYS glanced off the simple granite stone that Mom and I had placed on the grass in the southeast corner of the backyard. I had just finished shoveling dirt around the stone, and, although it was already autumn, sweat ran down my back. I handed her the shovel and asked, "Mom, why did you pick Apache?" I knew there had been six puppies in his husky litter, both male and female, and all were black and white. Mom paused as she put the shovel in the tool shed. I could see she was searching her memory to find the day Apache came to live with us, that rainy June day in 1980.

Mom lost her first dog, Pedro, a black Cocker Spaniel in the late 1950s. One day, he chased a squirrel across the street. She called him home and, as he was running back to her, a car hit him, and he died in her arms. Mom's second dog, Scamper, was a mixed breed mutt. With a pointed nose, pointed ears and reddish-colored fur, she looked like a fox. Mom found her at the ASPCA sometime in 1966, the year I went off to college. Scamper was a good companion until she died of old age in 1978. Mom was devastated but soldiered on.

After finishing college and graduate school, I worked locally and lived at home for a year. When I planned to leave New Jersey in the fall of 1980 to work in Washington, D.C., Mom feared the "empty nest" syndrome. One evening she said to my Dad, "You're at work all day, and when you get home, you just sit and read the paper. With Chris gone, who will I talk to now? Maybe I need another dog. We could go for walks together, you, me, and the dog."

Mom started visiting the local pet shop at the Rockaway Mall just outside the ground floor entrance to Macy's. Each time she visited, she would stop and tap on the windows to get the dogs to respond. Then she would come home and spend the dinner hour talking about this or that dog she had seen. That March, each evening while Dad read the paper, Mom was glued to the TV watching the Iditarod, the 998-mile dog sled race which runs across Alaska. The race pits twelve to sixteen dog teams against each other over an eight to sixteen day trek across a frozen wasteland and through storms of ice, rain, and snow.

After the Iditarod finished, Mom began to research the Siberian Husky. She often talked about how they were a chore to raise but well worth the effort. Huskies can be black and white, gray and white, or rust and white. Some have blue eyes, others have brown, and still others have one brown and one blue. Some people believe the blue eyes make them look colder and more like wolves with whom they share a family tree. Sometimes people are afraid of them, but they needn't be. Huskies clean themselves like cats and howl or growl rather than bark. They become extremely attached to their human families and very protective of them.

Mom told me stories about Huskies that she read in a dog magazine she borrowed from a neighbor. One Husky licked a dirty baby clean. Another sheltered a small child who was freezing. A third protected a family from thieves. She was in love. "On the other hand," she said, "they need a lot of care and attention. Even if there is a close bond, they can run away and not come back for days."

In June, a day before Mom's sixtieth birthday, Dad and I decided that Mom needed a new dog. Dad was a cat person and said, "I don't know why we don't get a cat. You don't need to take cats for walks. But I know your mother can't be without a dog." So on a gloomy Tuesday, we drove to Rockaway Mall. Mom wore her raincoat, but Dad forgot his umbrella. He and I ran full speed from the car to the Macy's entrance. We took the escalator to the pet store on the ground floor. The dogs, mostly purebreds, were locked in their cages. Some barked or whined or moved to the front of the cage as if to say, "Pick me." Others appeared tired, bored or just resigned to life in the cage. You just wanted to buy them all in order to get them out of there. Then we saw the litter of Siberian Huskies.

The pet store Siberians were all black and white with brown eyes. They put on quite a show wrestling, rolling, nipping, yelping, and splashing water at each other. My mom tapped on the window to get their attention, but they were too busy having a good time romping to notice.

One bright-eyed male pup got into all sorts of trouble. Occasionally, he looked up and stared as if he were saying, "Look at me. I'm the one you want." Mom wanted to take the whole bunch of masked marauders, but she could only have one. She commented on how the arrangement of white and black fur on their faces looked like masks or Indian war paint. After we brought him home, Mom named the one she chose, "Apache".

From that day forward, nothing separated Mom and Apache. They went for walks during the day. At night, he would sleep at the bottom of Mom and Dad's bed. Mom would talk to him for hours, play ball with him, and help him strengthen his baby teeth on a leather strap. Apache soon won over Dad. He would go on walks in the park with Mom and Apache on weekends and during the week when he had time. They would stop and chat with the other dog owners. After Apache got older and my dad retired, the two of them and Mom went to the park every day. It was a way to for Dad to spend time with Mom and get exercise especially after they got too old to play tennis.

Apache also adopted me. In some strange way, he knew every time I was coming home. He would begin to howl when my car was still a half mile away. Later, when I left Washington to work overseas and only came home at Christmas or Thanksgiving, he still seemed to know when I would arrive. Mom told me once that when she said, "Chris is coming," his ears turned forward as if he were on alert. He would sit by the window for hours, waiting.

When I married, he adopted my wife as well, and after my two sons were born, he cared for them as if they were his own. If they were dirty, he would sniff them and then trot over to my wife to inform her that she had work to do. When they were toddlers, the kids would often fall asleep with their heads on his back or stomach. He never complained if they stepped on him, even later, after he got sick.

Images of the past flipped before my eyes like a Rolodex of photographs chasing each other in a constant blur. First, Apache as a puppy, then full grown and later with two little blond kids, my sons, lying on top of him. Finally, I saw Apache with his head on Mom's lap when it was time to say a last goodbye and heard her whisper in his ear, "Run Apache! Run!"

I wondered if Mom had the same images running through her head. "He was a good dog," I said. I should have said more. Instead, I simply asked her, "Mom, why did you choose Apache that day at the pet store?"

Apache was so sick he could no longer walk and Mom had spent the last two weeks struggling to carry him outside to do his business two times a day. Mom's hands trembled as she shut the shed door. Her tired shoulders hunched over, and I stepped up to support her by putting my arm around her waist. As we slowly turned to walk back up the steps to the house, she said, quietly, "For the look in his eyes."

11
THE HOMECOMING

RUTH KNOCKED ON THE DOOR. A man with hazel eyes and a warm but troubled smile opened it. Ruth had not seen her husband Vincent for a long time, and he seemed surprised to see her. Forcing back the joy and pain, Vincent hugged her and quickly invited her into his sparsely furnished abode.

Bald on top with gray on the sides, Vincent appeared to be in his late fifties. At five-ten, he looked taller than Ruth remembered. He had put back the weight and muscle that Parkinson's had taken from him. His hands no longer quivered and his shoulders seemed straighter. The hollow indentations at his collarbones had filled in. She noticed he had regrown the mustache he sported when they were dating. It was in the Errol Flynn style, and she had loved it when they first met. The same old briar pipe with the smooth-finished bowl was stuck between his teeth, and she wondered when he had recommenced smoking. Vincent wore tan trousers and white stocks and still dressed in the same black tennis shoes with a Velcro strap instead of laces. He had switched to straps when the Parkinson's started to affect his ability to use his hands. Though his hands were steady, he apparently had gotten used to the laceless shoes. A white Lacoste polo shirt completed his outfit. He had never been a good tennis player, but he loved the sport, and she remembered all the times they had played at the club across the street from their home in New Jersey.

"Hello Vinny," she repeated. "It's been a while."

The living room had only a sofa and a comfortable looking armchair. A trombone stood on a stand in the corner. With no other visible furniture, it could have been anyone's living room, anywhere, anytime.

Ruth's naturally blonde hair was pulled back in a 1960s French knot, and she wore a purple nylon jumpsuit. Her hair no longer had the gray-white streaks that came after she stopped taking the trouble to color it, and she seemed a lot younger than Vinny remembered. She was more erect, her back was no longer bent, and she was not wearing the strong prescription bifocals that she had worn since the early 1980s. She walked across the room as energetically as she had when she danced at her son's high school graduation. Her smile had returned, and the sadness that hovered around her eyes, the last time they were together, was no longer there.

"You look comfortable here," she said. "Is that our sofa from the house on Boonton Avenue? By the way, you still don't believe you have a ranch in Texas, do you? Remember, you told me that the last time I saw you at the nursing-care facility. It was so sterile with the white walls and the hospital furniture. This is a lot nicer." Ruth removed her jump suit jacket, revealing her white polo shirt. She moved nearer to her husband, and they embraced for a minute like two people who have forgotten what it is to feel each other's warmth. A tear rolled slowly down Vinny's cheek.

"I've been waiting for you to come," he said. "It's been too long."

"It's been over thirteen years," she replied.

"Time seems to stand still these days, so I can't say for sure how long I've been here. I hope you can stay a while," he said. "Maybe we'll get a chance to go back to that beach on Fire Island. You remember. We went when Chris was a baby. All our friends were there. How is Chris, by the way?"

"He's doing just fine, and his boys are growing into wonderful young men. He calls me every night, sometimes twice a day. He and Liria are coming to see me today. When Mary learned I had left to see you, she called Chris and let him know I would no longer be there when he arrived."

Vincent looked puzzled. "Who's Mary?" he said.

"Oh, didn't I tell you?" she replied. "She's the nurse in charge of the retirement facility where I have been living. I've been there for about three years.

"Do you remember when you got sick and had to move to the nursing home? I went every day to see you, and we ate lunch together. All except for that one day. I had to leave to talk to the lawyer. When I returned, it was too late. It was probably for the best. You know I never liked to say goodbye. Every time I visited Chris and Liria in Virginia, I would just get on the train and wave as I was leaving but I never said the words. Each time they came to visit me in the nursing home, I cried when they left. Today was better; I left without saying goodbye to them. But they had the letter I wrote them before I went to the home."

Changing the subject, she said, "You seem well. You were so weak and sick the last time I saw you. That was just after your 82nd birthday. Those preceding four years were difficult for both of us. You look much younger now. Have you been exercising? I haven't been out much these last two years. Chris lives too far away to visit me more than once a month, and besides, he has a job and a family. After Apache left, then you, and my brother Richie, I've spent a lot of time alone with my memories wondering when I would see you all again."

Vincent sat down. "Funny, the things you remember," he said. "I remember mostly the good things and happy endings. Like the time you disappeared for hours on your way to your Uncle Herbert's home outside Charlotte, North Carolina. I was just about to call the state police when you called from Herb and Madeline's to tell me you had arrived. I think it was around ten at night. I was so relieved and so happy to see you when you got back."

"I made a mistake and got on Skyline Drive instead of Route 81, and then I was in the mountains and it got dark. I lost one headlight and couldn't see the exit signs. I was both lost and blind until that trucker pulled in front of my car, a real angel from heaven. He remained in front, led the way, and lit up the road for me until we got to Raleigh. After that, the drive to Charlotte was easy."

"Speaking of angels, how are my grandsons?" Vincent asked. "You said they are young men. I remember the last time I saw Michel. He played violin for me when I was sick. They all came to visit me at the nursing facility. Michel must have been around eleven or twelve then."

"Yes, and you clapped like you understood what was going on, the first window of clarity I'd seen in months."

Ruth paused, looking wistful. "Raphael is now twenty-six and Michel is twenty-four," she said softly. "They both graduated college, Raphael in 2010 and Michel three years after. Michel is in computer software design, and Raphael teaches history. They are now in Japan spending the Christmas holiday, so I would have missed seeing them this year, even if I had stayed. Looks like Chris and his wife, Liria, will have a lonely Christmas Eve without the kids."

"How could I forget?" Vincent said as he hit his head with his hand. "It's Christmas Eve. The boys will have a great time celebrating Christmas and the New Year in Japan. By the way, is Michel still playing violin?"

"He switched from classic to electric violin a few years ago and then stopped his classes," she said. "I think the best performance he ever gave was when he played for you that last time."

Vincent's body sagged a bit and he shook his head. "He really has talent. Too bad he decided to stop his studies."

"But he still accompanies his brother," Ruth said. "Raphael is quite good on the piano. Plays by ear. Last Fourth of July, they stopped by and played together for me all afternoon in the 'common room.' Attracted by the music, people kept coming by, and saying how wonderfully they played. I think the boys were pleased."

"You were at the nursing home for three years?" he asked.

"I was there three different times. After I broke my leg

the second time, it took a while to heal. I moved into the apartment wing a year ago and just left today. But I've wanted to leave for a long time. I miss our friends Katie and Joe, and my brother Richie and your sister Helene. By the way, have you kept up with your trombone? How about your dancing? Remember my Mom always called you the 'Latin from Manhattan' when we were dating and you came by to take me dancing."

"I've started playing the trombone again a while back. As for dancing, a while ago I decided the only good partner was you. Do you remember, in the 40s, when we used to dance to Tommy Dorsey and Glen Miller? I bet we could go dancing again. You're looking quite fit. I like the way you have your hair, the French knot. It's the way you wore it the day Chris graduated from college back in 1966. That was one of the happiest days of my life. Oh, by the way, I forgot to tell you. Apache is with me."

Ruth looked around, searching.

"He's back there behind the sofa, licking his fur like a cat." Vincent motioned to the corner with his head. "Strange how Siberians do that. Most dogs don't. We still go for walks every day at the Tourne Park near where we used to live; but we miss you. He still pulls too much, and I have to keep him on the long leash, or he'll disappear into the woods. Every once in a while he gets off the leash and runs but always comes back. I don't think he'd ever run away. He's too accustomed to being with me. Just like when he was with the both of us."

"Apache," Ruth called. The brown-eyed Siberian came bounding up and almost knocked her down, licking her face with pure joy. Ruth hugged the dog and then sat down on the floor next to him to pet him. "So his legs are better again? I missed him so these past years." Then turning to the dog, she said, "I've missed you," and tenderly rubbed his head behind the ears. "I remember how you used to act when you knew Chris was coming to visit. You would wait on the porch and watch for his car."

"Did you see that? His ears just perked up when you mentioned Chris's name. I'm glad you're here, Brown Eyes." Vincent said. "Let me show you around the place. It's small but comfortable."

"It's been years since you called me that, Vinny," she said, her voice trembling.

"I almost forgot. Your brother, Rich, came by to listen to jazz yesterday. You know I still have those vinyl records. He told me he had just played golf with Uncle Herb. You know how they love their golf. He is waiting for his wife Claire but she still has things to do and couldn't come yet. I think he knew you were coming today. I guess deep down, I knew too."

"Oh Vin, could we go for a walk with Apache like we used to? After he got sick, he couldn't walk, and I had to carry him outside. I remember the day he left, he had his head on my lap. I whispered my love and then he just went. Soon after that you got sick."

"Sure, Ruthy. We have all the time in the world. Meanwhile we'll walk, talk, and wait for Chris and Liria. After they got married, when they visited, they always came with us on our walks with Apache. I still remember fall in the state park with the grandkids playing in the piles of colored leaves and Chris and Liria walking in the golden sunset. Their visits were always too short. They'll be here

before you know it. This time I hope they'll stay."
"They'll stay," she said.

12

THE GIFT THAT WAS PARIS
(MISTRESS AND MUSE)

TAKING THE BUS FROM CHARLES de Gaulle Airport to Paris is still an electrifying experience. I feel a sensual energy, both physical and spiritual. The sensation is not always as strong as the first time, but when you have lived in Paris, you never forget her. Hemingway said, "If you were lucky enough to have lived in Paris as a young man, then wherever you go for the rest of your life it stays with you." I would add, when you return to her, the city you loved, left, and loved again, it is as if you have never been away.

Recently, I found a poem I wrote during my Paris years. It reflects the thoughts of a young man who, like Narcissus, gazes into the pool of his own emotions and is mesmerized by them. The poem captured a loneliness of the soul and brought a nostalgia for a lost time and place.

If I could pen my life in verse
And thus assure my place in time,
I'd sell my soul for all its worth
To write a short melodic line.
But I have not the wit nor style
To hold my readers for a while;
To bind them with my words' caress
And break the bonds of loneliness.

When I wrote the poem and showed it to my friend Frances, she said, wishing to encourage my aspiration to be a writer, "It shows great promise." Frances and Paris. Paris was my Aphrodite and my muse, and Frances my Minerva and guardian angel.

My Guide, Frances

When I lived there during the mid-seventies, Paris proved herself a hard mistress. Without a French government-issued work permit, I could neither work nor remain in France beyond a three-month limit. Every three months, I crossed the Swiss or Belgian border, had my passport stamped, and returned for another ninety days. Without a work permit, not even the newly arrived McDonald's fast-food restaurant would hire me. I applied for a job, after they opened in southern Paris, but the new French manager told me, "Impossible, Monsieur."

I met Frances the day I went to look for job advertisements on the bulletin board of the French American Cultural Center. An expat, Frances was teaching English for foreigners at this imposing stone building. Originally constructed in 1931 as a meeting place for expatriate artists, poets, and writers, it had become simply another location for taking English courses. Frances helped me survive my early days in Paris. She remains only a memory, but I will never forget her kindness.

Born to an English father and an American mother, Frances grew up alternately in Oxford and Chicago and moved to Paris in 1970. Sharing a mutual desire to write, be published, and become famous, we liked each other immediately. I needed to find a way to stay in Paris, and Frances had spent four years manipulating the system. She supplemented her poorly paid teaching job at the Raspail Center with freelance work providing private English lessons to executives. They introduced her to other French businessmen, allowing her to develop a large clientele.

Frances was attractive in a sort of Katharine Hepburn way. A tall and slender thirty-year-old with auburn hair cut in a "wedge" style, (bangs in the front, voluminous crown, and cut short on the nape), she chain-smoked like a *Parisienne*. She had mastered the art of sitting in cafés and making a coffee last an afternoon. As we discussed literature and watched people walk by, Frances would roll her lit cigarette in an ashtray, carving the burning end into a point,

A few days after we met, Frances invited me to her apartment located in a quiet neighborhood off the rue de Montparnasse in the fifteenth *arrondissement*. When I arrived, she heated some coffee on a propane camping stove, which she used for cooking. Her living room served as a bedroom and contained two mattresses stacked in one corner and a comfortable armchair and small refrigerator in the other. The bathroom was a toilet over which the owner had installed a showerhead with a drain in the floor in front of the toilet seat. You could see the naked pipes through a large hole in the wall.

This apartment, where Frances gave private English classes, was not far from the American Center. Most of her business clients had their offices near there. I would return frequently so we could discuss writing. One day while we were drinking coffee, Frances quoted Ernest Hemingway's book *Moveable Feast* where the author said, "Paris is a moveable feast." I was not familiar with this book of short stories but I never forgot that quote and soon learned what the author meant.

The Moveable Feast

Living in the "city of lights" on a slim budget meant avoiding expensive restaurants, nightclubs, and most theaters. Having made few friends, I was alone most of the time. However, Paris was my constant companion. The lights on the bridges over the Seine dazzled me. They sparkled like a crown of diamonds atop her raven hair. She mesmerized me with the exotic perfumes worn by passing French women. Most of all, each night, she served me a "moveable feast."

In the evenings, after I ended my unsuccessful job search, I'd grab a sandwich or croque monsieur at some café and then commence my exploration. I'd choose a different arrondissement each night and unwrap its sensual secrets slowly, much like a man would remove his lover's clothing. I rode the metro to a central stop in some neighborhood where the inhabitants and their interaction became my open-air theater. Sometimes I'd sit in cafés and watch people pass by. Other nights, I'd walk for hours, exploring each avenue and side street with the same intensity a detective would use when searching for a clue to solve a mystery. Paris was my mystery, and each night she revealed yet another clue about why she fascinated me.

I started my exploration in the Latin Quarter, best known to tourists. I had already visited the Quartier Latin during a visit to the famous university, La Sorbonne. A female Trotskyite named Marie was there most days, standing on the street near Jussieu. She carried a placard that protested the French government's oppression. She was petite with auburn hair that glowed like fire, and her blue eyes burned with passion when she discussed the "dictatorship of the proletariat" and "revolution." She tried to recruit me to her cause, and we promised to meet again. We never did, as I did not go back there during the day for many months.

As night fell, I returned to stroll along the Boulevard Montparnasse and the Boulevard Saint Michel. The many cafés, all clean well-lit places, closed around eight or nine. They were always full of bohemians and college students who then left to spend the rest of their evenings in jazz clubs, bars, and cheap Vietnamese restaurants.

After dark, the area belonged to street musicians like the black saxophonist who played at the Odeon metro entrance or the lonely female violinist and music student bewitching passersby with her classic pieces at the Saint Michel metro. Their music was not enough to satisfy my longing, but it made me forget my hunger.

Subsequent nights, I explored other left bank

arrondissements that were mostly dark with little movement. The American Cultural Center, where I had met Frances, closed at seven, except when there was some expensive concert or art exhibit. The area around Les Invalides, so crowded during the day with government workers and tourists, was silent and empty at night. Only the Eiffel Tower projected its light across the darkness like a lighthouse calling to a mariner lost on a dark sea. The fourteenth of July, French Bastille day, fireworks lit up the sky around the tower, les Jardins de Trocadero and Le Palais de Chaillot across the river with a temporary blaze of glory. Farther east, the Luxembourg Garden, popular for daytime strolls, was also dark and empty. Lights always burned in the many international student houses of the Cité Universitaire campus. But this university for foreigners did not belong to Paris and to those who struggled and dreamed there.

A Different Menu on the Right Bank

When I moved my odyssey to the other side of the Seine, I took the metro to the Georges Cinq stop. Starting at the Étoile, with the Arc de Triomphe in its middle, I walked east down the Champs-Elysées past expensive restaurants and chic hotels like the Georges Cinq. With its ornate windows, opulent rooms, cast iron doors, and elegantly clad greeters, the hotel and its majestic entrance welcomed wealthy patrons. I ended my wanderings where the Champs entered the Place de la Concorde. Sitting in some chic café for an hour or so, sipping a liquor or drinking coffee, I'd watch the passing women wearing outfits that made them look like models in *Vanity Fair* or *Vogue Paris*. The men in Italian suits, who accompanied the women, looked like they stepped out of a movie set.

Other nights, I moved farther down les Champs to the area around the Opera. Smaller, cheaper restaurants and cafés that stayed open until nine or ten filled this quartier. The Opera, with its domed roof, imposing statues, and white columns, shone like a pearl in the light cast by the streetlamps surrounding it.

This area was the gateway to my next discovery, Les Halles. French writer Emile Zola called this quartier "the belly of Paris," and it was full of quaint cobblestone streets, narrow alleys, and a large open-air day market. I visited once during the day and felt embraced by the interlaced essences of fruits and vegetables, the smell of fresh fish, and the perfume of incense and spices. The cries of "Oranges ici, poisson ici, fromage ici," added to the texture of this multi-colored masterpiece. Once the daylight disappeared, this neighborhood, still a feast of sights, sounds, and smells, appealed to a very different palate. The colors became more somber, the atmosphere seedier, and another cast of characters joined the stage. They brought with them a certain mystery, but I never stayed. I moved on.

Pigalle et Montmartre

If Paris were a woman, Pigalle would be the exotic lingerie she wore in bed. Aside from the Blois de Boulogne, there was nothing in all of nighttime Paris like Place

Pigalle. Unlike the Blois, which was not a place to be on foot, Pigalle was not dangerous. I exited at Saint Lazare and walked north on the rue Pigalle toward the Boulevard du Clichy. The rue Pigalle was a painter's delight. During the day, when sunlight glanced off the quaint buildings, there was a kaleidoscope of color. In the night's darkness, the colors disappeared under somber streetlights, which seemed like spotlights for a girlie show. The only color was in the cheap dresses worn by melancholy hookers. To avoid this street, I sometimes exited the metro directly at the Clichy stop. The prostitutes along the Boulevard du Clichy would still proposition me, but they were "high class" and dressed in fancy bustiers and slinky skirts. They'd ask, "Monsieur voulez-vous faire un party? Le Monsieur, veut-il faire la fête?" (You want to party?) They always used the polite *vous* form or referred to their potential customers in the third person.

Turning west from Clichy, I reached the famous nightclub Moulin Rouge on the rue de Veron. It was much too expensive for me, and the show on the street was just as good. It cost nothing to make a U-turn and walk east past the porno stores with their live sex acts, the titty bars, and the kiosks with girlie magazines featuring photos depicting various vivid sex acts.

While walking one night, I turned down a dark side street where a well-lit house shone alone in the darkness. It had a wide staircase leading to a majestic entrance. On the stairs were five women dressed in black in various stages of undress. Some wore black boots and leather; others sported stiletto heels and long lace stockings, still others wore baby doll lingerie or corsets with open tops to show off their breasts. Some appeared to be dominatrixes, with hats and whips and other accoutrements. I stared hard, but kept walking.

I could not shake the memory, so several nights later, I tried to find the place again. I thought I remembered the name of the street, or at least where I turned off the Boulevard de Clichy, but I never found it. It had disappeared into thin air. Paris can be like that. Often, it's better not to unwrap certain gifts or pursue stranger mysteries.

As I climbed the hill behind Clichy, the white neo-Byzantine basilica, L'église de Sacre Coeur rose like New Jerusalem reaching upward from Montmartre to the heavens. With her artists' shops, outdoor painters and potters, and uneven cobble stone streets, Montmartre spread her arms around the church like a nun embracing the Holy Grail. But Montmartre was no nunnery, just a sort of purgatory, an antechamber, a stepping-stone from Pigalle to Sacre Coeur. I drank, talked to the artists, and listened to live music in this neighborhood full of small restaurants. Picasso had been a regular at Au Lapin Agile. Toulouse-Lautrec and Renoir preferred Pigalle. Maybe they were right.

Shakespeare and Company

When I asked Frances to suggest a place where I could write, she told me about Shakespeare and Company. I had heard of it but had not yet read Hemingway's *Movable Feast* with its chapter devoted to the bookstore and its proprietor, Sylvia Beach Whitman. The first time

I went to the location on Rue de la Bûcherie, I purchased Hemingway's book and read it on the spot.

It was not the original bookstore where Hemingway and others borrowed books. That one disappeared in 1941. George Whitman Beach, Sylvia's nephew, opened the new place in 1955. The store's bookshelves rose from floor to ceiling. There were chairs and tables for customers to sit and write or read for hours. The clerks always stamped a picture of William Shakespeare and the words "Paris, ground zero" inside the book covers. The bookstore faced the Seine and the Ile de la Cité. A tall hedge blocked the view, but if you moved down a bit, you could see the Paris boat dock and Notre Dame towering above.

Surviving Paris

Frances found me my first real job in Paris. A small private company that hired native speakers to teach English to French executives employed me and paid in cash under the table, so it did not have to pay taxes. As it never recorded the payments made, it could hire people without work permits. After several weeks, management fired me. They caught me speaking French to their clients because I needed to explain complicated rules of English grammar. Madame la Directrice scolded me severely. "Monsieur, on ne parle jamais avec les clients en Français!" (Never speak to them in French!)

Several days after I was fired, Frances mentioned a job interview she had seen advertised on the bulletin board at the American Cultural Center. At the interview, a fit, military-looking man showed up to talk with six of us. Well dressed and wearing a tailored pinstriped suit and dark tie, his muscles rippled under the tight sleeves, and it was obvious that he was a man of action. During my interview, he asked me if I had traveled to Africa and if I knew how to handle weapons. He then met with the group as a whole and told us to return the same time the next day. Five of us returned. The mystery man never showed up, nor did the sixth member of our group. We all figured number six was the one he chose. If the rumor that the recruiter was a mercenary or "soldier of fortune" were true, I was glad he had not chosen me.

In desperation, I wrote to my mother in New Jersey and told her about my job predicament. She sent me an excellent suggestion. "Why don't you go to grad school?" I told Frances about the idea. She approved and added, "As a student, you can obtain a student visa and the right to work legally for twenty hours a week. You won't have to leave the country every three months." I favored the idea, especially when I discovered that if I were a student, I could try out for the University of Paris tennis team.

Several weeks passed, and I went for an interview at the *École du syndicalism* (Contemporary History) department of the Sorbonne. My interview, in French, with Le Professeur Jean Droz, lasted fifteen minutes. I explained my U.S. master's thesis on French Communism and Socialism and asked when I could take the entrance exam. Professeur Droz quickly answered, "Vous l'avez passé." (You just passed it.)

I joined the Sorbonne tennis team and started practicing in an unheated tent-like facility at Roland Garros, home of the French Open. Tom, a fellow American from California, was taller and bigger than me, and with his well-placed serve, excellent volley, and quiet, low-key temperament, was the perfect doubles partner. The French knew absolutely nothing about doubles, and we usually had little difficulty defeating our opponents. The coach was impressed.

Prof du Tennis

After a month, the coach introduced me to his good friend Antoine Costaux, a burly Frenchman from Nice who ran a judo academy. The coach knew I had taught tennis for several years in the U.S. and vouched for me with Antoine. The academy had a full-size tennis court on the roof. Blond-haired Antoine, who sported a handlebar mustache that made him look like Archduke Ferdinand of Austria, hired me on the spot as the academy tennis instructor. When I got to know him better, I learned that Antoine served in the French army, spent some time in la police de Paris, and after mastering several martial arts, opened his own academy. His dojo, a garage-like building, was located on a small street in a working-class neighborhood.

My first student, Marie, a forty-something French housewife, had never held a tennis racquet. She had two kids in a nearby French lycée and a husband who worked at the French railroad company SNCF. She kept her peroxide dyed red-blond hair under a cap, wore white Capri pants and a yellow t-shirt. After I explained the basics of the forehand, I tossed her some balls. Instead of keeping a firm wrist, she turned her wrist upward, and her balls lobbed over the tall wire fence surrounding the court and bounced off a couple neighborhood roofs before falling into the street and disappearing. She quickly depleted my stash of used tennis balls but finally got the hang of it after several weeks. Then we would lose only one or two balls per session. Other students I taught included local children and women but no men. Working class Frenchmen did not play tennis. Tati, another housewife, usually wore a small, tight bikini top and short shorts when she came to her lessons. She was always afraid of breaking her fingernails. Her outfit had no place to put a spare tennis ball, and when she tried to place a ball inside the back of her shorts, she definitely caught my attention.

Professeur Droz et les Communists

Named for the famous pro-Moscow post-war French Communist Party leader, Maurice Thorez, the institute where I did my research, was located on a broad avenue in the southern part of Paris. Every day, I went there to read old editions of the official party newspaper, *L'Humanité.* My goal was to discover how the party elite used ideology to purge opponents.

Paris is damp and dreary in the winter, like a love affair gone cold but which lingers on. Most Parisians who have the means leave to ski the sun-filled mountains of the Alps. After four frustrating months of reading old newspapers in an icebox of a room with one radiator and only a lamb's wool jacket for warmth, I was back in Professeur Droz's office. French professors met with their doctoral students once or twice a year to make sure they were still alive. At the start of the meeting, Professeur Droz asked me why I was wasting my time reading L'Humanité. I did not have the courage to tell him he had suggested it. He agreed with my proposal to research *Cahiers du Communism*, a party magazine devoted to ideology. That worked better, and from my research I soon learned that the party leaders used certain buzzwords for people whom they labeled ideological heretics. In reality, these words could be attributed to anyone the party wanted to excommunicate. It was a great way to get rid of one's enemies.

Moving On

Antoine, my boss at the judo academy, was not a communist or even a socialist, but he wanted to make sure his working-class neighbors could afford tennis lessons. He did not let this interfere with his goal to make a good profit. After weeks of minimum payment for my efforts, we parted ways. Again, I was without a job, but the future appeared bright when Frances suggested I apply at the American School of Paris. They did not have a teaching position for me, but fortunately needed a tennis coach.

With my research at the institute and the new commute to work, I no longer had time to spend writing at Shakespeare and Company or visit with Frances. That spring, she decided to go on holiday in the south of France. We promised to keep in touch and get together when she returned, but it never happened. I never returned to the Raspail Center and never saw her again. A new phase in my life had begun.

13
MICHAEL AND THE TRIP TO NICE

"HEY MICHAEL," I SAID, **"WHEN** did Jean say we're going to begin hitchhiking to Nice? He mentioned something about leaving from the Port d'Italie. Have you told Chantal you're going?"

We were sitting in our landlady's living room. It was a large house in the Paris suburbs, where each of us rented a room. Michael looked up from opening the letter I had just given him. "We're supposed to be there tomorrow at nine in the morning and meet Jean just outside the metro station," he replied. "We'll all try to catch a ride from there. Jean says there are tons of drivers going south."

An Annapolis junior, Michael was near the end of his year abroad studying at the Université Catholique on the Rue D'Assas in Paris. When the academic year finished, he planned to return to the Naval Academy for senior year, receive a commission, and be assigned to a ship.

Michael had studied French in college for two years while I had four years in undergrad school, then two in my Master's program and had been in Paris for a year. Although my French was better than Michael's, I had neither his good looks nor his talent for making friends, especially with French girls. Speaking French was still difficult, though I could understand perfectly. The conversation always seemed to move on before I thought out what I wanted to contribute. Michael, however, was an extrovert and got by in spite of his poor French because he charmed everyone whether in English or French.

We first met our mutual friend, Jean Leblanc, at the Catholic University's student center. Jean was French and in his second year at CU. Short and stocky, he had sandy hair, brown eyes, irregular teeth, and a pockmarked face. I liked Jean very much, but he was more Michael's friend. Jean was an introvert like me and innocent in the ways of women. He adored Michael and wanted to be more like him.

With his trained baritone singing voice, blond hair, and blue eyes, Michael was quite popular at his university and at local Paris nightclubs. Several nights a week, instead of studying, he would go out with Charles Luc, the wayward son of our landlady Mme. Roulle. The two frequented different nightclubs in the sixteenth arrondissement where they trolled for women, partied, and got drunk. They would return in Charles Luc's sport Peugeot, racing full speed along the Seine passing the Pompidou Hospital to the Peripherique, which runs around Paris, then take back roads to Meudon and Mme. Roulle's house. Michael met his girlfriend, Chantal, an Air France flight attendant, at one of these clubs. Although Chantal meant Jane in English, Chantal was no "plain Jane."

At times Michael reminded me of the white-hot electric light that draws moths to it, singes their wings, and lets them fall to the ground. One night, he was supposed to meet Jean for dinner in town, but he never showed. Later he told Jean that he had gone to dinner with Chantal. Another time, he and I agreed to see a movie in the Latin Quarter. I waited an hour in front of the theater. He never showed. Chantal had invited him to the Lido, and Michael "knew I would understand." Another afternoon he invited me to have coffee with him and Chantal at a café in the sixteenth arrondissement near Trocadero, as Chantal rented an apartment nearby. Michael never showed, but at least I became better acquainted with Chantal.

Chantal seemed like a sweet, simple girl who was caught up in the glamorous life of an Air France flight attendant. She loved the international travel it afforded her. Another flight attendant, whom I met, told me that in spite of the seeming excitement of international travel, her life was just like being a waitress except at a higher altitude and with a better-looking uniform. I did not see it then. I only saw Chantal, with the physique of a model. Maybe because she was not mine, she mesmerized me. When she dressed for work, Chantal was the perfect image of the hôtesse de l'air in the Air France TV advertisements. Along with her blue uniform, she sported the pageboy blonde hair. Her eyes were light blue, she had the perfect smile, wore Dior perfume, and used red lipstick. Her sexy French accent when speaking English added to the allure. Who wouldn't fall in love with her?

As the sun set over the garden outside Mme. Roulle's spacious living room, Michael was still looking at Chantal's letter and deciding whether to open it. For some reason, he seemed hesitant once he realized it was from Chantal.

Earlier that afternoon, Chantal had found me at my favorite Latin Quarter café, Les Deux Magots in Saint-Germaine-des-Pres, the heart of the Latin Quarter. Chantal knew I loved the place because I had told her that it had been the haunt of expatriates and existentialists. The likes of Ernest Hemingway and James Joyce, Albert Camus, Jean Paul Sartre, and Simone de Beauvoir were patrons in the years between 1914 and 1950.

They called it Les Deux Magots because of the two statues of Chinese mandarins or magicians, which graced the original lingerie store. In the 1890s, the store moved to a new location and became a café. The café was designed in the form of a soft triangle, and the building had a square front and diagonal sides with full floor-to-ceiling glass windows. Outside there were tables with hunter green umbrellas matching the building's green awnings.

The croque monsieur, melted cheese and ham on toasted bread with béchamel sauce, croquet madame, add an egg, and the various croissants, baguette sandwiches, omelets, salade niçoise, with tomatoes, eggs, tuna and green beans, and the "ot dogs" were excellent. I went there because the café au lait was hot and strong, and the Deux Magots was just a short walk up the Boulevard Saint Germaine from where I studied.

Chantal marched into the cafe, found my table, and immediately took a seat. She handed me a letter in a somewhat mysterious manner and said in a choked voice,

"C'est pour Michael, si te plaît." (Please give it to Michael.) She then stood up and ran out the door. I thought she might have been crying.

The afternoon sunlight was disappearing outside the large living room window when Michael finished reading the letter. His face turned white, and he threw the letter on the floor.

"Michael," I asked, "what's this all about?"

"It means I'm not going to Nice with you guys," he responded. "Chantal claims she is pregnant and going to have my baby. I think she is just blackmailing me, as she knows I will be leaving in four weeks and I was trying to break-off with her before the summer. Why didn't you tell her I had already left for Nice? She didn't know you were going along, and she would have believed that I had already left. Now, I have to stay and solve this. You and Jean go to Nice!"

"Could she really be pregnant? She seemed so sincere and so upset; she was crying."

"You're so naïve," he responded. "French women want to get their claws into you and never let go!"

In silence, I looked at Michael. He did not know I was secretly in love with Chantal. When she came into the café, I probably could have said that Michael had already left, but she was troubled. I only thought about her. Jean and I would have to go alone. Michael had to figure out his life, hopefully, without hurting someone else. He assumed she was not pregnant. I hoped so, for her sake.

The next morning at nine, I met Jean at the Port d'Orleans metro exit. I was wearing street shoes, khaki summer pants, and a polo shirt and carrying a travel bag on my shoulder.

Jean, more prepared than I, had on tennis shoes, a hat, and jeans, and carried a warm jacket. We stepped out onto the Autoroute du Sud and put out our thumbs. Five hours later, we were still in the same spot. A truck driver finally took pity on us. He was going to Grenoble by way of Dijon. Grenoble was east to the mountains and Swiss border, not south towards Nice and the Cote d'Azur. At that point, we just wanted to get out of Paris, so we climbed aboard.

We knew we were near Dijon when we began to pass fields of mustard plants with the sun-colored flowers. They looked like a golden-yellow carpet undulating in the wind. After we passed Lyon, we continued southeast to Grenoble where the driver ended his journey. It was dark, nine o'clock at night, and we were hungry. We bought a baguette and some ham and cheese, which we ate along with some mystery soup we got from a roadside café. The soup was a mistake.

It was getting cold as we waited at the truck stop for a ride. Finally, around ten p.m., we set off into a Grenoble suburb to find a place to sleep. After walking for about twenty minutes, we found an abandoned house and a door that opened to a cellar under the house. It was a lot colder than I expected. May, in the French Alps, is damp, and we had no fire for heat. I put on all my shirts and a light jacket that I had brought with me. We lay on some cardboard as protection from the cold ground. It was then that the food hit me. I think it must have been the soup. I went outside to relieve myself in the cold night air and cleaned-up with a newspaper I had found in the cellar. There was no water around to use for washing. Afterwards we huddled together and tried to sleep.

The next morning, frost was on the grass but the sun shone brightly as we walked back to the main road. With our thumbs out, we began to follow the old Route Napoleon. After several hours of walking, we noticed signs for the town of Gap, the capitol of the Hautes-Alpes department. We had not counted on the distance and the mountains. At some point, one of my street shoes lost a heel, and I started to limp. Just outside of Gap, a truck stopped for us and gave us a ride to the red tile-roofed town situated at 2,406 feet above sea level on the banks of the La Luye River. This time our wait was only an hour. Another trucker, who was going to Nice, offered to take us. As the truck descended the mountains, we passed fields of purple lavender that looked like waves of an impressionist sea.

By that time, we had been walking and hitching for two days. I had a pronounced limp. It was late afternoon, we were hungry, and we needed to find a café where we could get a hot dog or croquet monsieur and coffee. The strong coffee woke me up and got my blood running. The sun felt delicious as we sat near the window with the afternoon rays warming our backs.

The first order of business was to find a place to stay. A waiter at the café recommended a local pension a few blocks away, near the train station. We immediately went there and got a room, breakfast included, for forty-five francs, the cost of an inexpensive meal in the U.S. We got the cheaper rate because it was still off season. After a hot shower, we felt human again and slept well that night.

We were up early the next morning. After a breakfast of croissants, myrtille jelly and cheese, we strolled to the beach. Beginning at the western end of the famous palm-fringed Promenade des Anglais, we followed the road along the beach and around the bay to the Quai des États-Unis. We finished at the old port, flanked on both sides by eighteenth century red-ochre buildings. The bay was dotted with yachts and the port was full of restaurants. We dined on oysters and drank Orangina and white wine. In the afternoon, we walked back to the Promenade des Anglais and swam in the Baie des Anges. The water was clean and cold but the beach was rough with pebbles and stones.

The invigorating swim prepared us for the long walk back to the dirty train station and our life-worn but clean pension. We arrived with our clothes dripping-wet with perspiration from the walk in the afternoon sun. You could smell the purple lilac in the air. The scent was not spicy and intense like the Asian variety but heavy and sweet. After a shower, we changed clothes and had dinner at a quiet nearby café. We both chose the sea bass with lime. Jean drank a light white wine and I had Perrier. We went to bed tired but happy.

The next morning, we caught a train to Cannes. The city didn't have Nice's quiet charm but it was a favorite of the European jet set. The Boulevard de la Croisette qualifies as Cannes' Promenade des Anglais. In early May, Cannes was just warming up for the famous Festival International du Film, which brought the finest of American and International cinema to the theater. We passed the open air Cinema de la Plage and decided to swim in the cold aqua blue Mediterranean. After window-shopping for a good inexpensive menu, we ate Coquilles Saint Jacques at a modest restaurant.

That afternoon, we hitched back to Nice. The traffic stopped dead along the winding highway that runs west through the hills, and we were actually moving faster on foot than the cars. The occupants cheered us on with the football chant, "Allez! Allez!" but no one offered us a ride. Several miles outside of Nice, we finally got a lift to the train station, recovered our bags from the pension, and caught the train to Marseille.

We arrived just in time to catch the nine p.m. to Paris. The comfortable seats facing each other and the total privacy afforded by the glass doors closing off each compartment made me feel like I was on the Orient Express. Jean took one side and stretched out. I took the other. We arrived in Paris with tired legs but feeling somewhat rested.

The next morning, I ran into Michael who was eating breakfast in Mme. Roulle's kitchen. He did not look happy. "How are things?" I said. "Did you straighten things out with Chantal?"

"I met her the day after you gave me the letter. She cried a lot but finally admitted she was not pregnant. I spent the next two days with her but she was impossible. I finally told her I was leaving earlier than planned and going to Italy before returning to the U.S. I'm leaving after my course ends next week. I think I'll go to Venice, then Rome and Napoli. I want to see where I could eventually be assigned. If I get the Mediterranean assignment after graduation, my ship will probably dock near the U.S. Navy base in Napoli."

I was going to tell him about my adventures and the trip's disasters, but he didn't seem in the mood to listen. He was preoccupied with avoiding Chantal and the places they used to meet. He knew she would not show up at Mme. Roulle's, as she did not know the address.

Chantal could not find Michael, so she found me instead. Two days later, I was at my favorite table at Les Deux Magots when Chantal walked in and took a seat. "Tu sais," she almost spit out the words. "Michael est un salaud! Il a fait des promesses… Je croyais qu'on s'aimait. Il m'a abandonné!" I got it. Michael was a bastard. I was stunned by her open declaration that Michael had abandoned her when she loved him and wanted to be with him. My heart went out to her, but there was nothing I could do. I could have told her that I loved her, but she hadn't noticed before so why would she care now? I did manage to get out the words "Si je peux t'aider en quelque chose?" a weak offer of help, but I could tell she did not want to see anyone who had anything to do with Michael. It was too painful. I just listened when she said in lilting English, "I do not think we shall meet again. I just wanted to say goodbye," and then she walked out the door and out of my life.

Michael left the next week. Months passed and my foot healed but my heart did not. A year passed, and then another. I had not really known Chantal that well. Maybe I was never in love with Chantal, herself, but with an image of beauty or maybe beauty itself. Whatever it was, I never got close enough to singe my wings.

Three years after Michael left Paris, I finally heard from him. A mutual friend helped him track me down. I was spending time with friends in Washington, and he was visiting his parents in Rockville, Maryland, just outside the city. He had graduated Annapolis, been assigned to a ship based at Naples, and had brought his Italian girlfriend, soon-to-be bride, to meet his mom and dad. We met for coffee. He introduced me to his fiancée, an outgoing, pretty, dark-skinned girl from Rome. With her long, dark hair and tanned skin, she was quite different from Chantal. Of course, I didn't bring up Chantal in front of her. I did not want to spoil the reunion.

Michael got what he wanted. His life had worked out just as he had planned. Nothing got in his way. It didn't matter that there was a broken heart left behind. I hope Chantal finally forgot Michael. It hadn't taken him long to forget her.

14

THE AMERICAN SCHOOL OF PARIS

IN FALL OF 1974, SEVERAL months after arriving in Paris, my money began to run out, and I put my writing ambitions on hold while I looked for a job. When I began my studies at the University of Paris, I discovered that as I was a university student, the French Government would allow me to work twenty hours a week. Having run through several illegal temporary jobs, I decided to apply for a part-time teaching position or substitute-teacher job at the American School of Paris.

When I visited the school, the secretary in the main office told me I could leave my name but said, "Frankly, we don't hire teachers locally, and we already have a full list of substitutes." By some grace of fortune, Bob Lemay, Director of Athletics, stopped by while I was speaking with the secretary. A six-foot-four French Canadian with the large arm muscles of an oarsman, Bob sported a pirate mustache, which complemented his long, dark, wavy hair. When Bob spoke English, he ended each sentence with the invariant tag, "Eh." He spoke French like a Quebecois, and we got along immediately, speaking both in English and in French. After we discussed my background as a tennis coach in the Washington, D.C. area, he seemed interested in my working at the school. I appreciated his interest but thought nothing would come of it and quickly forgot our conversation.

From Instructor to Tennis Coach

Several days before the Christmas holidays, Bob called and left a message with my landlady who was unhappy she had to take a call for me. I was completely surprised when I returned his call and he said, "As you know we have a multipurpose bubble for tennis, volleyball, and basketball. I would like to start a tennis club and hire you to give private tennis lessons to students, parents, and faculty. You can use the school bubble over the winter holiday and then on weekends during the school year. You can also stay on as tennis coach in the spring. I want you to start this coming Friday, Christmas Eve."

Bob offered to put a flyer in his office to advertise my availability and an announcement in the school weekly newspaper. "Since you don't have a phone, you can set up classes on the spot with those who stop by."

That Christmas Eve was the loneliest in my life. I was accustomed to spending Christmas with family or friends. Most of the American and French students and the expats I had met over the past months had gone home for the holiday or fled rainy Paris for skiing in the Alps. I began my first day on the job by siting in the cocoon-like white bubble for six hours with my racquet and tennis balls for company and a bottle of Orangina, a baguette, and some cheese as my companions.

The bubble, unlike the covered clay courts at Rolland Garros where I practiced with the University of Paris tennis team, was heated and had a velvet-like surface. There were white lines for tennis, gold lines for basketball, red lines for volleyball, and blue lines for indoor soccer. Just figuring out which lines went with what sport made my head hurt.

Tired and bored, I sat on the ground because there were no chairs. Just before four in the afternoon, Peter Hawkins, a diplomat from the American Embassy stopped by. Peter told me his kids attended the American School, and he wanted lessons for them and himself. The kids were currently on vacation and they all were ready to start lessons on Monday, in just two days.

Saturday, Christmas day, I was again on the floor in my white cocoon, eating a baguette and ham, when another client arrived. John Silverstein, a math teacher at the school, paid me fifty francs on the spot for an hour lesson and scheduled another for the next day. Although John originally appeared to be an answer to a prayer and took several lessons a week during the holiday, he turned out to be only interested in helping himself.

For the first six weeks, I made great money until the newly formed "teachers association," headed by John, decided they would take over the tennis club and exclude non-members, those who were not faculty or relatives of faculty. This, of course, excluded the new tennis pro, me, and my clients! John set himself up as the instructor for the "members" and quickly put me out of business.

Fortunately, my new friend Bob Lemay, school athletic director and crew coach, came to my rescue. Bob invited me to lunch at the school cafeteria and offered me another job. "Écoutes, why don't we just start tennis season early. I know the weather is bad, but you can train your boys and girls in the bubble after school." I thus became the official American School of Paris tennis coach, and we started training the second week in February.

A Better Form of Transportation

In those days, it was not possible to get directly from one Paris suburb to another without changing trains and waiting for a connecting train. I lived in a southwest suburb. In order to be at school for my job as tennis coach, I took a train to a southeast suburb. Then I waited an hour for my connection and took a second train to the American School in Garches, a northwest suburb. This was faster than going into Paris and back out again, but the trip took all morning and included a fifteen-minute walk to the school gate.

After a few weeks, I got tired of spending a good part of my day traveling and used the money I had earned from my several weeks of private lessons to buy an old motorcycle. I purchased it from a used car dealer in downtown Paris who forgot to tell me how to shift gears. I tried to shift by engaging the clutch without cutting the throttle. The bike wouldn't shift out of first, emitted a groaning noise that made it sound like a dying animal, and I was forced to listen to this moaning sound all the way home. A French neighbor, who saw me arrive slowly and painfully, told me to cut the throttle, pull in the clutch, shift gears, and then engage the throttle.

Commuting to work on the cycle cut my tortuous travel time by two-and-a-half hours. I discovered that if I rode north and through the Parc de Saint Cloud, I could quickly arrive at the school. After I ascended the steep hill and entered the park, I would put the bike in fourth and could feel the brisk morning air and the cold wind in my face. When the weather was clear, nothing could compare with the thrill of speeding by the forest, soccer fields, and walking paths. The sense of freedom was incredible, and it was as if I were flying.

The Boys Team

On the first day of practice, I met with my newly formed boys' team in the tennis bubble. I was lucky enough to have Peter, a senior from New York City. He was redoing his last year of high school in Paris before applying to a college in the U.S. Peter was staying with his father, an executive who was separated from Peter's mother. While his mother remained in the U.S., Peter's father decided to bring him to Paris so they could spend more time together. However, he spent long hours at his job, and Peter, feeling abandoned, was more than willing to stay long hours after school. An athletic teenager with a strong serve and excellent volley, Peter became the lynchpin of my men's number one doubles team. He was nineteen but with his beard and mustache, Peter looked twenty-five.

I paired him with Kevin, a skinny, baby-faced junior

who had long brown hair and liked math and motorcycles. Chad was the third member of my tennis triumvirate, a junior who had transferred from New Jersey. Chad was ranked in the Middle Atlantic States in the U.S., and I soon chose him to be my number one singles player. I rounded out the team by selecting another five players to whom I assigned the number two and three singles slots, a backup singles slot, and the number two doubles position.

Bob told me we would be up against the American School of London whose team practiced at Wimbledon. Our two other principal opponents would be the International School of Brussels and the Brussels American School at Sterrebeck. Both rented court time at a local indoor facility outside Brussels. With the cold rainy weather and only one indoor court for practice, we ran drills, and the team members played matches only in their spare time. We were at a significant disadvantage, so we started early and made every day count.

Every March during spring break, Bob took his crew team to Tours to practice racing their shells on the two rivers surrounding the city. Tours provided more opportunity for practice than Paris where it was hard to schedule time on the Seine. Bob invited me to take the boys tennis team as well. He informed me, "Tours is situated in the Loir valley several hours from Paris. We'll stay outside of town at a university housing complex which is now empty after the construction of newer dorms. It's pretty basic, but they have two beds to a room and showers down the hall. The facility has two cement tennis courts, and you can use them for the week. I'll be practicing all day on one of the rivers with my team, but we can all get dinner together at the end of the day."

Tennis in Tours

On a cold March Monday, we boarded one of the school's buses and left for Tours. The Cher River to the south and the Loire River to the north surround the town. The François Rabelais University, named after the satirical writer of the fourteenth century, had relocated downtown, but the university still owned the old campus, located across the Cher in Montjoyeux. We there stayed there for the week.

With the crew team now out on one of the two rivers, I set up a morning and afternoon schedule for my team. Our two courts made of asphalt were dotted with craters, had uneven sloping and nets that needed to be propped up. The depressions in the court surface quickly filled with water when it rained, but fortunately we had only one bad day. I divided my eight boys into two groups of four. I gave each group a series of backcourt, service, and net-volley exercises. Apart from eating at the university cafeteria, they were either on the tennis courts or in bed. By the end of the week, after training eight hours a day, their tennis looked much better.

The Friday before we returned to Paris, I was making the night rounds and could not find Peter and Kevin, my first team doubles players. I finally convinced the other kids to tell me where the two had gone. They had taken a cab to a Friday night porno movie shown in an outdoor soccer stadium.

Hurrying to Bob's room, I knocked loudly. As he opened it a crack, I could smell French perfume in the background.

When I told him about the boys, he closed the door, grabbed some clothes, and we set off for the stadium. I never saw his female companion.

Bob commented with a smile, "Your boys are taking the Rabelais stuff too seriously. It's not going to look too good to the Headmaster. Let's resolve this quietly."

We divided the stadium with Bob on one side and me on the other. People in the audience were yelling "Asseyez-vous," as I wandered up and down the aisles, trying to avoid stepping on feet or interrupting amorous couples. I don't remember the title of the film, but I saw enough to know it included a pool scene where a buxom naked young lady threw a cowboy hat onto the erect member of a guy who was skinny dipping.

After about twenty minutes, we found the two boys deeply engrossed in the film. We hustled them onto the bus and soon returned them to their dorm room. Peter, the older of the two, freely admitted that he had been the instigator. He was an honest kid but had a penchant for stretching limits and sometimes breaking rules. I believe it had to do with the fact that he felt abandoned by his father. Bob and I quickly agreed that we would not mention the incident back at school, but the two would do some after school chores around the athletic office.

London, Brussels, and the League Final

We played our first away match against the American School of London. Arriving on a stormy Friday night, after taking the train and boat across the channel, we checked into our hotel and got ready for the next day. It rained for two days and the tournament was a wash. I spent two days with the kids, touring London, getting lost and talking to Scots and Londoners whose English I could not understand. The food was atrocious, and we never got to play at Wimbledon. Later, we made several bus trips to Brussels where we played separate matches against the American DOD School and the International School of Brussels. Although the team had some difficulties, we felt strong and looked forward to the Four-Way Tournament held at a tennis club outside Brussels.

After several rounds, the only two teams left in the Brussels Four-Way were the American School of Paris and Brussels International School. It would be a fight to the finish with three matches in all. Chad won his first singles match, but Peter, who I chose to play singles and doubles, lost the second singles match to a boy who floated the ball and drove him crazy. Everything centered on the doubles final, with winner take all. I began biting my fingernails. Kevin and Peter were to play for our school. Kevin had not yet played and needed some time to warm up. I took Peter aside and told him that he was the captain, and he should hold the team together.

Peter served like a demon and was unpassable at net. Nothing got by him. Kevin was nervous and needed some time to gain confidence. The score after an hour and a half was one set each. I called the two boys off the court and said, "Don't let it get to your heads. Focus on the ball and play like it's a practice back at school." The last set went six to six and then our boys won the cliffhanger by two points in a tiebreak.

The boys had done it. They won the trophy against three

schools whose teams had more money, more court time, and more experience. They were ecstatic. I even let Peter drink a beer on the way back as we drove to Paris, celebrating all the way. It was the first time the American School of Paris had won this tournament. Later, there was a special awards ceremony in the auditorium with the Headmaster handing out appreciation medals. Bob Lemay beamed and was beyond himself with joy.

The Girl's Team, Another Cup of Tea

What the girls lacked in talent they made up for with spirit and good humor. They were all sophomores and juniors except for Tina, a dark-haired, blue-eyed senior. At eighteen, she was just five years younger than I was. She became my number one girls' singles player. One time I was in the gym looking for the girls and happened to pass the girls locker room. I got enough of a view of Tina getting dressed to let me know that if I was not careful, I could get in deep trouble. Fortunately, she had a boyfriend and was not interested in anyone else. I didn't have to face a temptation that could have gotten me fired.

Linda, a blonde junior, and May, a short, stout sophomore with close-cropped hair, had some tennis experience, and they became my girls' first-string doubles team. The rest of the girls had little experience, and it was quite a challenge to get them up to speed. In those days, the boys always took precedence, and Bob told me to give the boys the majority of my time.

The girls usually played against both American and International school opponents on our school courts at our campus outside Paris. We also played some local French girls' teams from lycées around Paris. Our girls were having fun learning tennis but producing mixed results. This went on right up to the All International Schools' tournament in June.

The girls played this year-end tournament in Brussels at the same indoor facility in Serrebeck where the boys had played and won a month before. The other three schools involved were the American School of London, the Brussels DOD School in Serrebeck, and the Brussels International School in Kattenberg. Bob decided to send us by train. I went alone with my team of six girls because no parent volunteered to chaperon, and Bob had a Saturday crew race on the Seine. I told him, "Don't worry. I can handle six girls for a weekend. The two Brussels host schools have offered to house the girls with parents of their tennis team members as chaperones."

As the train pulled out of the Paris Gare du Nord, I was dealing with team baggage when Tina exclaimed from inside the cabin, "That's really gross!" In the background, someone else screamed hysterically. When I entered the cabin, I found Tina, May, and Linda staring out the window at a French guy who had dropped his trousers and was masturbating. He smiled at the girls and stuck out his tongue as our train pulled by. Two of them turned away. May continued screaming but did not turn away. I finally got everyone calmed down, but that wasn't the last of my difficulties.

Within two-and-a-half hours, we pulled into Midi station, downtown Brussels. The Serrebeck School had sent a van, and we all piled in and set off for the suburbs.

As we passed the gilded city center with the Grande Place, ornate-columned Town Hall, gothic baroque Bourse, and the House of the Guilds, the girls chatted endlessly as they pointed at the buildings. Within less than an hour, we arrived at the seventeen acre Serrebeck campus.

Our team reported to the reception area, and the tournament staff began assigning host families. Three of the girls simply went with their escort to find their host family. However, I faced a rebellion from Tina, May, and Linda who claimed they were too old to stay with families. They wanted to stay with me in the small three-star pension and restaurant in downtown Brussels where Bob had reserved my room. Two of the girls said they knew their parents would approve and one said she already had her parents' permission. Being young and stupid, I allowed them to con me into agreeing. As we drove to downtown Brussels, I remember thinking, "It's just one night and we'll be on the train back to Paris Saturday evening."

The four of us had a wonderful dinner of haricot vertes, pomme frites, and steak with a special sauce. I was accustomed to Parisian bistro and café food so for me it was a culinary delight. The girls wanted to drink wine, but I finally put my foot down and said, "No!" After dinner, they all came to my room to watch TV. Fortunately, that's all that happened, and I sent them to bed at ten o'clock as we had a big day awaiting us.

The next day, the other three girls played against the International School of Kattenberg. They lost. However, Tina, May, and Linda beat their opponents from the DOD School of Brussels. The London School had one win and one loss, so we ended up playing them in the finals.

We lost both singles, but maintained our pride when Tina and Linda took the doubles match and allowed us to finish second overall. It was a moral victory for a team that had barely known how to play tennis when the year started.

Back in Paris on Monday afternoon, Bob called me into his office. "What were you thinking letting three girls stay in a hotel with you? Two of the parents were furious. Fortunately, all the girls said nothing happened, so you're off the hook. Don't ever do that again." Bob quickly forgot about the incident when I showed him the second-place trophy the girls had won. He tried to get me to promise him another year as coach, but he knew I had decided to move on. It was time for a change. With the season over, I decided to visit my folks in New Jersey.

The Dangerous Trip Home

In searching for a cheap flight to the U.S., I found an Air Pakistan flight that originated in Karachi and made a stop in Paris. There was only one catch. My ticket would read Karachi-New York but I would be going through customs and boarding in Paris. I went to the airport with some trepidation but boarded without a problem. Once on the plane, I assumed the excitement was over. I lay back in my seat and went to sleep. Suddenly, some sort of alarm awakened me.

Looking back down the aisle, I saw two Pakistani men trying to cook their dinner by lighting a small pile of sticks in the center aisle of the plane. They had pots and pans which they intended to put on top of the fire. The flight attendant rushed over and began pouring water from a plastic bottle on the fire. She was screaming at the men, calling them idiots, and telling them to put away their utensils and return to their seats. After that, I could not get back to sleep and was extremely happy to arrive at Newark airport, still alive.

Time for a Real Vacation

After two weeks in New Jersey, I missed Paris and was glad to return. This time though, I decided to take a break from my studies. I saw an advertisement for sports instructors for Club Med and decided to apply for a position as a tennis coach. I interviewed at their main Paris office, and they soon assigned me to a club in the south of Italy. I spent the next six months listening to the Italian kids refer to me as maestro. I always thought that term referred to orchestra conductors and was flattered by the title. But that is another story.

15
THE CLUB MED

L'arrivée

THE CLUB MED IN OTRANTO sat on the heel of the Italian boot and looked across the Adriatic Sea toward Albania. When I arrived there in the summer of 1976, the first person I met was Mirdieu. That was his stage name. His real name was Pierre, but he had seen the name Mirdieu in a Dumas novel and decided he liked it. With his three-cornered hat, his German handlebar military mustache, and baggy clown pants, Mirdieu, as club social director, played the part of a court jester or village buffoon. As he took my bag and walked me to the boss's office, Mirdieu filled me in on the responsibilities of a tennis GO, gentil organisateur.

Marcel, the chef de village, waved me into his office in an imperial manner. His long hair, black mustache, tattoos, and goatee made him look like a gangster from Marseille.

He was indeed from Marseille, and I soon learned that in Club Med, a chef du village has as much power as the "Godfather." I assumed Marcel's slightly dismissive welcome was a sign of contempt for a foreigner, but I later learned that he had been both busy and preoccupied when I arrived. He quickly introduced me to his deputy, Stefan, so we could discuss details of my employment. I immediately distrusted Stefan, a greasy French Moroccan, who tried to break my fingers with his grip. It was Mirdieu, with his warm smile and comedic style, who became the ledge my fingers could grasp to avoid falling off the alien and potentially hostile mountain I was now climbing.

It had been a long trip from Paris. Our connecting plane in Rome had engine problems, and we were bused overnight from Rome to Bari and then on to Otranto. It was too dark to see any of the Italian countryside, so I spent the time reminding myself that I needed to follow the guidance given during my two weeks of tennis training at Club Med's Pompadour Centre D'Equitation in south central France. It didn't matter that I had spent my youth playing in tournaments and then taught aggressive American-style tennis in Washington, D.C. for four years. The French clay court style was to stay on the baseline, hit looping topspin balls, and never, never go to net. I knew I would have to get with the program or not last long.

Realizing I was exhausted, Mirdieu showed me to my room. It was located in one of a series of brick structures located next to the open-air men's showers. They reminded me of the showers in my high school gym's locker room, except our gym's showers were indoors. The women's quarters and their showers were on the opposite side of the small GO compound. As we were workers, not guests, we did not merit the well-furnished, comfortable rooms with an indoor private shower and balcony. My room had a bunk bed, a chair, and a table in the corner where I could put my suitcase.

My roommate, Denis, another tennis instructor, had taken the top bunk. Denis was at dinner so Mirdieu suggested we go to the dining hall where we would find him. As we walked, the sound of music drifted across the air. I recognized the song, *Maladie d'Amour*, which was written somewhere in the French Caribbean in 1933. The 1976 version had become popular in Paris that year. The music relaxed me and turned my thoughts to the six months of fun I expected to have in this paradise. I remember the words.

"Maladie d'amour, maladie de la jeunesse… car l'amour c'est la mort, mais c'est aussi la vie. Car l'amour c'est la mort et c'est le paradis." (Love is youth's sickness. It is life, death, and paradise.)

Les Hôtesses

The dining hall felt like I had entered the gates of paradise. A bevy of goddesses greeted the guests and seated them at various tables. Mirdieu guided me to the GO table near an enormous buffet. I thought, *My sleeping arrangements might not be the best, but at least I will eat well!* There were plates of grilled steaks, chicken, lamb, and pork chops. The smell brought back memories of my family's backyard barbecues except that we grilled only hamburgers. A multitude of salads, leafy green with red juicy tomatoes, green and red peppers, and black and green olives, and grilled vegetables such as eggplant, broccoli and squash, accompanied the meat and poultry. The guests served themselves at the buffet, but the hôtesses, in their see-through gowns or pareos and bikini tops, brought the drinks including wine, fruit juices, and sodas.

Management had hired these women for one reason. They all were gorgeous. I later learned their names and some background. Danielle, a blonde with cornflower eyes and milky skin, was a Parisian who breathed sophistication and snobbery. Olivia had ample breasts accompanied by perfectly tanned skin and ginger-colored hair. Chrystel, another blonde, came from the south of France. She would have made a female porn star envious. Raven-haired Marie had speckled olive skin and wanton eyes. She was Stefan's petite amie.

In the end, they were all unapproachable, at least for me. Not that I didn't try during the next six months. Maybe it was because I put them on a pedestal or because they put themselves there. The two blondes made me think of dreams I had as a child; of a fairy princess that I, Prince Charming, would somehow conquer and make my own. When I mentioned my frustration to my roommate Denis, he just laughed and told me to set my sights lower. He commented with sarcasm, "Quand on est amoureuse d'elle même, c'est impossible d'aimer un autre." (Their self-love prevents them from caring about others.) He was right; they were actors, infatuated with their image in the mirror, and wondering how they looked in this or that light, if their lipstick was just right, and if they showed enough cleavage. Denis let me in on another secret. "C'est amusant," he said.

"Elles sont amoureuses de quelqu'un qui n'aime pas les femmes." (It's funny, they're all in love with someone who is gay.) I shared his sense of irony.

Marie the hostess and Stefan the deputy chief were an item but soon appeared to separate. When I passed her on the way to my tennis lessons, she looked sad, like she needed company, but I couldn't stop to talk. Denis, as usual, was au courant and said in French, "Don't even think about it. She has a venereal disease and I think Stefan gave it to her." So much for that option. Even though the club did not allow drugs, Marie and Stefan had been into weed and possibly some coke. As time went on, I spent my time teaching tennis, taking siestas when it was too hot, relieving my sexual tensions by myself, and eating as well as I could.

Les Trois Mousquetaires

They called Abdul, Denis, and me the three musketeers. It was either in reference to the Dumas book or in homage to the four Musketeers of French tennis history who dominated the game during the 1920s. You could never have found three people who were more unalike, but we all loved tennis and had each other's backs. Dennis, tall and thin with a pencil mustache and a Lyonnais accent, was young and quiet. His French was warmer and much slower than the machine gun Parisian French to which I was accustomed. He was adept at the French clay-court style of tennis and drove me crazy when we played. Abdul, technically a Muslim, was Senegalese with charcoal skin. With his dark eyes, sparkling white teeth, crew cut, constant smile, and jovial manner, he reminded me of a gentle panda bear. Although he was originally assigned to teach sailing, management transferred him to the tennis squad after a few weeks. Abdul's African French had a special lilt that spoke to me of places I had never been; of shark-infested seas and pirate ships that once roamed the African coast.

One rare day when we did not have to teach, Club Med set up a match for us against a local Italian club. We arrived at their courts in nearby Lecce and found that their number one player was formerly ranked number three in all of Italy. The three of us briefly huddled together. "Who's going to play number one?" I said.

Abdul replied, "Let me do it. I'm going to lose anyway. Maybe you two can still win."

Denis' opinion won out. "Fais ce que tu fais toujours," he told me. "You have the biggest serve and best volley. Just do what you always do, serve hard, charge net like a crazy man, and hope he can't pass you. If he goes to net, use your big forehand and pass him."

"It's settled," I replied. "I'll do my best." Although it was one of my better serving days, my opponent hit the ball past me every time when I came to the net. His hard topspin dipped the ball at my feet before I had a chance to volley. When I tried to pass him at the net, he handled my hardest ball by deftly dropping it over the net. It was a total humiliation. The other two fared only slightly better. We ended with handshakes, hugs from the Italians, and plenty of wine and spaghetti.

From that time forward, the three of us were inseparable. We ate together, were on the courts together, and drank together in the evenings. After several weeks, Denis found his true love, at least for that summer. She was a well-endowed girl who worked in the finance office. She had been interested in me and I introduced her to Denis. I guess it was because she did not meet my standards. She was not a hôtesse, not blonde, and not a goddess, but she was sweet, kind, and good to Denis.

Abdul did not have time for a girlfriend. He was in bed with a different guest almost every night. Most of them were older German women who were attracted by the fantasy of sleeping with a black African male. At one point, Denis and I took him aside. "Look Abdul," we said. "Don't you know these women are just using you and look down on you behind your back?"

Abdul only smiled that panda smile which told us he was satisfied with himself. "Don't you guys know that I am using them? So we are even." He went on letting the women take advantage of him.

Roberto le grand

Roberto was a good friend, and there was a strange symbiosis between us. He took the role of the older, more experienced Don Juan, and I ended up as his apprentice and admirer. Not a day passed when Roberto didn't have a story about his previous night's conquest. He hailed from the Isle Saint-Marqueritte off the coast of Cannes and was currently a judo instructor. A weight lifter, he loved to show off his muscles, and we often talked while I was on a work break and he was pumping iron. Roberto's receding hairline concerned him. He believed he was going bald, but he had convinced himself that bald men were more virile. He often said, "Les femmes, elles aime quelqu'un qui sait comment faire au lit." (Women love someone who knows what they are doing in bed.) He was probably right about that. Experience in bed was certainly a point in his favor. However, I often wondered how much of one's self-worth could be built on sexual prowess. Deep down, Roberto was a lonely man. He desperately needed a friend or maybe just a sympathetic audience before whom he could validate his self-worth.

One night when we were drinking and he had consumed two bottles of wine, he became morose. "Qu'est-ce que je vais faire après?"

"What do you mean? What will you do after what?" I said.

He responded in French, "After the Club Med. All summers end, and I have been working year-round, going from one Club Med to another for ten years now. How much longer can it last?"

Not knowing what to say, I looked down at my drink. I knew I would leave after my six months ended and return to Paris, my friends and my life there. What did Roberto have? "I don't know," I said. "Maybe you could open a judo school somewhere in France?"

"J'espère. I hope you're right," he replied and fell silent. I hope he finally found his safe harbor.

Etienne, le maître de la mer

Etienne was tall, with long blond hair, a perfect nose, soft blue eyes, and all the hostesses wanted him. He was a sailing instructor from Martinique, an island in the French Caribbean. When he was not sailing, he spent most of his time playing guitar with the band of reggae types who hailed from Isle Maurice, off the coast of Africa.

Otranto was like that. It pulled together instructors, musicians, and drifters from the far reaches of the former French empire, from Africa to Europe, the Caribbean and Arcadia. What everyone had in common was the French language. Although we were in Italy, almost everything was done in French; proof that the French empire had not died.

For a while, you would never see Etienne without a crowd of gorgeous females around him like a rock star. Etienne was always gracious. He could have had his pick of any of them. I am not normally a jealous person but I must admit to envying his physique and the power he held over women. They became the moths and he was the flame who could singe their wings. But after a while, the women drifted away. When I asked Denis why, he simply said, "Etienne n'aime pas les femmes. Il s'interesse aux hommes." After learning of Etienne's sexual preferences, I understood why they had all drifted away. Somehow, the irony made my frustration even greater.

La Suisse Bien Nue

Most beaches in the Mediterranean and the Adriatic are made of rocks and stones, not sand. Otranto was no exception. Those instructors who had traveled from Polynesia or the Caribbean said that what Otranto had was not a beach at all. They all complained that the Italian sun had replaced the bronze color of their skin with a strange olive coloration. They would arrive looking like Greek gods and goddesses tanned to perfection, and they would begin to look like yellow-green Italian olives after a few weeks in Otranto.

I think what first caught my attention was her atypical bronze tan. She was completely naked and her body had no bikini lines. All the men coming back from the beach would stop and talk to her. I wondered how they did it. Their Speedo swimsuits barely covered their privates in a non-erect form. Fortunately, I was wearing shorts so I stopped to talk without fear. Her name was Aimée, she was Suisse Romaine and spoke French. She filled her conversation with Swiss colloquial expressions like *septant* instead of *soixant-dix* for seventy. During our short chat, in which my eyes keep wandering to places they should not have gone, she agreed to meet me that evening for drinks. When I arrived at the bar, ten other guys were waiting for her to appear. Apparently, she had invited half the male population of the club. She never showed.

Mirdieu

Late summer arrived, and it was almost time for my departure for Paris. During lunch one day, I sat at the table next to Mirdieu, and as he started to speak, his body seemed to sag and his ever-present smile was gone. "What's wrong?" I said. "Are you sick?"

He sighed. "It's not what you think, a sickness of the body or la maladie d'amour."

Memories of our first few days together flashed through my mind. I, the only American at the Club, desperately wanted to fit in. Seeing this, Mirdieu invited me to accompany him on his daily social rounds. I joined him as, dressed in his three-corner hat and baggy pants, he marched around the village. He had a metal kazoo and would hum silly tunes, make outrageous jokes, offer people drinks, juggle three balls, and do anything to keep people happy.

After a few weeks, Marcel, the Chef de village, singled me out at one of our weekly meetings for my esprit du corps. He praised me and commented, "I thought the American was making fun of us all with his checkered British cap and shorts. But he is okay, un bon type." I knew Mirdieu was behind this praise.

These weekly meetings stopped about halfway through my stay. As the weeks progressed, Marcel became more of a recluse; staying in his office and running the place more and more like a mafia don. We never saw him. He just sent Stefan to give us orders. For most of us, nothing changed. We did our jobs, taught what we were supposed to teach, and life went on. There was no longer any village spirit, but that's just the way things were.

For Mirdieu, it was different. He bravely soldiered on, but this atmosphere affected him the most. Beneath all the buffoonery and sarcasm, he actually cared about others. Morale was low and so was Mirdieu's life force. It was hard to be around him. He had become a sad copy of himself, a pathetic organ grinder playing a melancholy tune.

My last week, I could bear it no longer. I fled to the "children's village" where female monatrices took care of the kids so their parents were free to indulge in more adult pleasures.

Les monatrices d'enfants

As I climbed the hill to the children's club, I heard the

sound of a guitar and kids singing. Florence met me in the courtyard with a warm welcome. Most of the girls who worked there were dressed in jeans or shorts. Florence had her hair tied back and wore no make-up. She offered me the guitar, and I played some James Taylor tunes I had learned while in college. I became an immediate hit. Florence chastised me. "Why is first time you come to visit us? C'est vraiment domage hein!" I also wondered why I had never gone there before.

After I spent all afternoon and into the evening singing with these young women and kids, I felt like myself for the first time in six months. The women were interested in American music, politics, and culture. Most were students spending the summer working at a vacation resort, because, like me, they did not have the money to take a vacation. They had homes, families, and lives awaiting them. I remembered then that I too had a life waiting for me. That life did not include pareos, beaches, and tennis, but graduate school, a real job, and friends who knew who I was.

Le retour

Three days later, I left for Paris. Florence, who was with me on the Paris flight, took a connecting flight to Bordeaux. We lost touch. Abdul showed up one night several months later, knocked on my window, talked my ear off, and left Paris the next morning for the Club Med in Senegal. For months after, every time I heard "La maladie d'amour" on the radio, I would think of Otranto, paradis et mort, and I was glad I was myself again.

16

MICHEL NO HABLA

Some choose silence to attract attention while others choose silence to avoid it.

Welcome to Republica de Salemoga

"NEXT TIME I MAY NOT be so lucky," she said. "This is the second time I've been stopped by the Salemogan state police on my way to the Embassy. Both times they accused me of driving with a non-valid license plate and demanded I pay a U.S. fifty-dollar fine. Other wives who have foreign license plates have also been falsely charged with the same violation. The police always go away when you pay them the amount they want. When am I going to get my diplomatic plates? It's already the end of August, and we arrived in late July."

"They're coming soon," Tom replied. "I spoke with the guy who's in charge of all the admin stuff, and he assured me we'll get one set of dip plates."

His answer didn't reassure his wife. Although Tom had Salemogan plates on the secondhand car he bought after arriving, his wife needed a set of dip plates to protect her from police extortion. Tom preferred local plates to avoid being a target of kidnappers, narco-traffickers, and terrorists. This was a strange paradox; what protected her would put him at risk.

His wife Sheila continued, "Today I told the police officer that I would not move until someone came from the Embassy. When I called the Embassy so he could discuss it with them, he quickly lost interest and left."

"Welcome to Salemoga," Tom said. "Two years to go until we leave. We'll just have to get used to things as they are."

Hoping to segue to something more positive, Tom asked, "So how is Michel doing at Montessori?"

"I think the school is good for him," she said. "The classes are small, and he gets one-on-one time with his teacher. But everything is in Spanish. The teachers only speak a bit of English."

"He'll adjust," Tom said. "Small kids pick up languages quickly."

"It's not that," she said. "It's been four weeks since we arrived, and they say he hasn't spoken a word. All I hear is 'Michel no habla.' Then he gets in the car with me after school and you can't shut him up. He talks all the way home. When I ask him why he won't speak in class, he just looks at me with those brown eyes and gives me that apple-cheeked smile like an inscrutable Japanese elder."

"He's only four and he's shy," Tom replied. "Give him

some time."

"I don't think he's shy," she replied. "He's getting a lot of attention from the teachers, and the other kids think he is something special. 'Michel no habla'. They all say it. He is something special for them."

"He's not the only one not speaking," Tom said. "Today, a group of us from the Embassy went to talk with the police chief about corruption, crime, and narcotics. According to the chief, everything is fine. Even the lower grade officers will not talk to us. What else should we expect? We're asking them to be honest, brave, and do their job. The narcos are telling them they can keep their lives and the lives of their families and get money on the side if they just look the other way. All we have to offer is the possibility of making Salemoga a safer and better place."

At that moment, Tom suddenly remembered he needed to be back at work that evening and asked Sheila, "Can you ask Minerva to close the gate for me when I leave? I've got a reception at eight tonight."

Their home, located in the crime-ridden downtown barrio of Puerto Pimento, the capitol, did not have an electric gate. When they arrived at night, they had to do a drive-by, scope out the area, do a U-turn, drive by again, stop, and Sheila would jump out and open the gate. Once the gate was open, Tom would quickly drive in. Sometimes she drove and he got out.

Tom usually took a bus to work, but as it was evening and dark, he decided to take the car. As he left the house, he realized he was already late for the reception and had forgotten it was his no-drive day. Puerto Pimento, with bus and car exhaust emissions, was one of the most polluted cities in the world. Riding in a taxi without air conditioning guaranteed a good dose of carbon monoxide. The view from above the city or while driving up the mountain revealed a dark cloud covering all below with a grayish haze. The Salemogan government's solution was to ban private cars from driving one day a week. Tom's day was Thursday.

As Tom drove past the first traffic circle, a police officer standing by his car motioned for him to pull over. He pointed to Tom's license plate and said, "Hoy es Jueves, el señor esta en violación de la ley. El señor necessita pagar una multa." (Today is Thursday and you can't drive. You have to pay a fine.)

Trying to get out of the fine, Tom quickly said, "Embajada de los Estados Unidos," and pulled out his Embassy ID. The policeman ignored the ID.

Tom thought, *What he really wants is una mordida, a bribe.* So he asked, "Quanto es la multa?"

"Lo que el señore quiera," the officer replied. They went back and forth and finally settled on fifty dollars in pesos. The officer looked pleased and said he would follow Tom to the Embassy so he would not get another ticket. Once they reached the gate, he yelled "Vaya con Dios," and drove off.

Later, Tom learned that only the ecological police, who wore different uniforms and were on foot, could issue tickets for driving on a person's no-drive day. The police officer who had stopped him had no authority to issue an ecological ticket.

Lost Sweaters

One day, Sheila was going through her clothes. She had

stopped wearing her contacts because of the dust and fecal matter that rained down on Puerto Pimento from the hills above, and she was still not used to her old glasses. She was looking for two hand-knit wool sweaters from Uruguay. "I've looked everywhere," she said.

"Have you asked Minerva?" Tom replied.

"Yes, but she wouldn't say a thing. She just looked guilty."

"Ask Judith," he said. Minerva, their live-in maid, stayed in a small room at the back of the house along with Judith, her ten-year-old daughter. Due to her mother's Indian blood, Judith was dark-skinned, with dark brown eyes and braided black hair. She loved to play games with Tom's two sons. She was a smart girl and in some ways wiser than her mother. Judith could certainly budget better and do math.

A little later, Sheila returned. "I asked Judith and guess what? Judith told me that Minerva washed the sweaters in the machine, and they shrank. She even showed me where Minerva hid them so I wouldn't find them."

Tom offered a "hum" and said, "I hope that girl never grows up to be like her mother, but it doesn't look like she has much of a chance. Maybe we should raise Minerva's salary so Judith can attend a better school?"

Sheila frowned. "That would be like rewarding Minerva for her dishonesty." They left it there.

A Rolex for your Life

One afternoon, John, Tom's coworker at the Embassy, came back from a lunch break, looking pale. "What happened?" Tom asked.

"You know I park my car in the parking annex across

from the Banco de Salemoga. I went out after lunch to get my gym clothes. The police car, which is always parked on the street next to the lot, was missing and the parking attendant was gone. Just as I reached my car, two men approached me and asked for my Rolex. I hit the first but the second put a gun to my head. They took the Rolex and all the cash I had in my pocket. Fortunately, they didn't ask for my credit cards."

John was six-two with sandy hair, blue eyes, and a brown mustache. He was in good physical shape, with the physique of a football guard and could easily hold his own in a fight. The end of the story did not surprise Tom. He knew strength meant very little when faced with a gun to the head.

"John, why in God's name did you go out wearing a real Rolex?" Tom asked. "I wouldn't even wear a fake one. I don't want my wrist cut when someone tries to rip it off my arm. You're lucky to be alive!"

"Yeah," he said, "I should have known better, but I'm leaving tomorrow for home and I wasn't thinking."

Of course, when the Embassy security team went to the site, they interviewed the local guard and he had seen nothing. There was no explanation as to why the police car was not in its usual place next to the lot, and the parking lot attendant claimed he had gone on lunch break, and his replacement had not shown up.

Danger Everywhere

John's story was one of many stories Tom heard over the next months. There was Marco, a Mormon friend, who had gone with his family to church in the southern area of the city. After lunch, they stopped at a local McDonald's. Unfortunately, they chose the wrong fast-food restaurant. Three masked gunmen robbed everyone in the restaurant, taking money and valuables. Marco lost his credit cards as well.

Sheila's friend Ann stopped at a light in the traffic circle near a prominent landmark close to the Embassy. She had her pocketbook on the seat next to her. In a matter of seconds, two youths broke her passenger side window and grabbed her purse. Another wife customarily wore an expensive ring and had her finger broken when a youth grabbed the ring from her hand while she was waiting for a cab. Fortunately, he did not cut off her finger.

A U.S. Department of State Employee visiting the Embassy for a week was told to take only taxis called by his hotel or a restaurant. He went to dinner in a busy section of Puerto Pimento not too far from the Embassy and decided to walk back to his hotel. Unfortunately, he hailed a passing cab. Within seconds, the cab stopped abruptly causing him to bump his head on the front seat. Two men leaped in and put a gun in his side. They drove him to a barrio near the airport, beat him, made him strip, and told him to give them his credit cards. He only had one card with him and handed it over to them. Fortunately, they did not make him accompany them to a nearby ATM. While they were gone, wearing only undershorts, he jumped out of the car and ran down the street, only to come face to face with a group of gang members. They wanted to know why he was in their neighborhood. The gang members took pity on him, put him in a taxi, and sent him back to his hotel. He survived with only a broken nose and two broken ribs. He had given the robbers a false pin number for his credit card, and he canceled the card when he got back to his hotel.

The local foreign diplomats group decided to sponsor a weekend trip to see old colonial mining towns. Tom wanted to go but his boys were sick so he and Sheila begged off. The other diplomats flew to the west side of a mining valley and boarded a tourist train that ran from one side to the other. Somewhere during the trip, the train stopped, a group of armed masked men boarded, and they took all the passengers' jewelry, money, and credit cards.

Even a drive down the road that ran along the shore to beautiful beaches was possible only by driving during the daytime, and Tom learned never to stray into the mountains for fear of robbers or revolutionaries.

Clothes and Weddings

Tom's family life continued despite daily challenges. His older son Rapha attended Westburry Institute, a private school located in an old mansion in the middle of a local park. The student body was composed mostly of the sons and daughters of high-level local officials and businessmen. Rapha had to wear a uniform of dark pants and a hunter-green blazer with a "W" insignia. A blond-haired, white, turquoise-eyed boy dressed in an exclusive prep-school uniform would have drawn a high price on the Salemogan black market, so Tom walked him to the bus every morning, and Sheila picked him up in the afternoon.

One day Rapha came home without his jacket. "Where's your jacket?" Sheila asked.

"I must have forgotten it at school," he replied.

"First thing tomorrow, go to the lost and found and retrieve it," she ordered.

The next day he came back wearing a jacket that was dirty and too big for him. His jacket had been well tailored and cleaned every two weeks. Sheila went to the school and asked why they couldn't find *his* jacket. She explained that she had put a label inside with his name written on it. The woman in charge of the secretaria simply said, "I don't know what to say. Los niños siempre pierden cosas." (Kids always lose things.) Sheila left enraged but helpless, unable to penetrate the culture of dishonesty even among the rich.

Tom and Sheila's younger son, Michel, was still at Montessori. He was doing well academically but still not speaking. He had a girlfriend, and they were to be married. Everyone knew they were a couple. She, a local girl going on four, and he, a silent, American-Brazilian going on five, had a wedding in the classroom during dress-up day. She wore a white veil and white lace gown. He wore a gaucho hat, pants and boots like the cowboys in Sheila's home state. There was a big party with a white cake, and all the kids got involved. Of course there were no vows because "Michel no habla."

Death and Politics

One morning, a year into their stay, Sheila called Tom from the living room. "Come quickly," she yelled. "You've got to see this!"

Not knowing what she was talking about, Tom stepped into the room. The television news channel was covering an assassination. He assumed it was another priest or policeman. A cardinal had been killed that year at a major airport and a federal police inspector investigating state police corruption had been shot dead in the north of the country. Drug lords or corrupt police were suspected of ordering the hits. Now they were referring to a presidential candidate.

As Tom listened, a reporter mentioned a Salemogan Revolutionary Party (SRP) presidential candidate who was killed. Reading off his teleprompter, he said, "Pablo Martinez, candidate for the SRP was shot dead by a lone gunman while he was attending a campaign rally on the streets of Puerto Pimento. The perpetrator was a disgruntled machinery worker, Mario Alverez." The candidate's security team had allowed the perpetrator to stand next to the candidate and pull the trigger. Tom remembered John and Bobby Kennedy, and tears filled his eyes.

Martinez was the bright hope, the John Kennedy who would change the Presidency and represent the "people of Salemoga." With his dark mustache and equally dark but receding hair, he projected strength and wisdom. The members of the candidate's campaign team told Tom that he would clean up the party, get rid of the old corrupt politicians, restore human rights, fight narco-trafficking, and bring Salemoga into the land of economic stability. Tom thought it all sounded so credible.

Nevertheless, the candidate had many enemies in and outside the party, including the old guard, the current President's brother, and narcos and criminal elements. In the following days, conspiracy theories abounded. It was the narcos. It was the president's brother. It was the "old guard." The lone gunmen was a fall guy, an Oswald, who may not have even pulled the trigger. The party put up another candidate who was not well known. The SRP still had power so he was elected and the Salemogan money's value dropped by half vis-à-vis the dollar.

Earthquakes and Lost Hope

Several weeks before the assassination, Tom was having breakfast with a senator who was Martinez's speechwriter. He and the senator shared a common European educational background and often discussed local politics. The senator laughingly referred to a previous breakfast several weeks prior. "I'm surprised you agreed to come back to this place after what happened before."

"You mean the earthquake?" Tom said. Tom remembered they had been sitting in the restaurant situated in the basement of a downtown building when the large glass ball lights suspended by wiring began swinging back and forth. Looking around, the two noticed that all the waiters had left without saying a word. They decided to leave and, arriving at street level, noticed that the ground shook for a few minutes but nothing fell.

At this breakfast, the senator spoke about his hopes for the future. "Martinez is sure to win," he said. "Ya lo creo. Es su destino. He is a new type of politician, an economist with an MBA from overseas. He will fight for the peoples. He will end corruption."

And Tom believed him.

Coming Full Circle

During the years until their departure, Tom and Sheila

saw one scandal after another as the economy sank, corruption abounded, the army sold weapons for profit, and the narco-traffickers became more powerful. They did not know that life would come full circle. Tom, Sheila, and the boys drove out of the Puerto Pimento at four in the morning, hoping to reach a neighboring country in time so they could drop their car and catch a plane for the U.S. Within minutes, a police officer stopped them. "Your car is overcrowded with baggage and you are on a main highway at four in the morning," he said. Fortunately, Tom still had his diplomatic credentials and said, "Do you want to call the Embassy?"

"Andele," he replied, and they began the drive out of Salemoga toward the neighboring country.

Puerto Pimento had been a mixed experience for the family. Raphael left the country never having found his original school blazer. Sheila left without having received an illegal traffic ticket or being accosted on the street. Tom left with the memory of good, honest friends who had seen their hopes dashed with the assassination of a candidate. Michel left without ever speaking in school. He spoke to the maid, the gardener, and the repairmen, but he needed to protect his reputation at school, to be seen as special. He had become a "Salemogan gringo" both in his language ability and in his proclivity for knowing when to speak and when to stay silent.

17
THE ASSASSIN SCHOOL BUS

"We can judge the heart of a man by
his treatment of animals." Emanuel Kant

*AS THE DIPLOMATIC-PLATED CAR moving toward
downtown Zarpathia stopped for a traffic light, a motorcycle
pulled alongside. At the light where the car had stopped, a low
stone wall separated the inbound lanes of Mikhanoria Avenue
from the outbound traffic. The European army attaché driving
the automobile did not hear the motorcycle approaching from
behind nor see it stop on his left. He was oblivious to the woman
passenger who was sitting behind the driver until too late. At
that point, there was no escape. He could not move his vehicle in
any direction. The dividing wall blocked him to the left and cars
blocked his right. Had his vehicle been armored, the bullet she
fired would not have pierced the car's side window and shattered
his head. He died in a matter of seconds as the motorcycle passed
with the driver continuing to weave between the lanes of traffic*

until he was out of view. The Adrian Marxist terrorist group "Free Adria Movement" had made another hit.

A New Home in Zarpathia

When Tom discovered that his next overseas assignment would be with the U.S. Embassy in Zarpathia, his family began to read all they could about Adria. They looked forward to visiting historic places and living in Zarpathia the capitol with an ancient citadel at its center. They leapt at the opportunity to live in a location that had had so much influence on democratic tradition and influenced so many generations.

Tom and his family arrived in Zarpathia on a hot August day. Their embassy-assigned house was situated across the street from the Air Attaché's home in a residential neighborhood. A split-level with a kitchen in the basement, the house sat on a small property with a garden. The grapefruit trees produced abundant, edible fruit, but the beautiful and enticing wild orange bushes along the fence-line yielded oranges that left a sour taste in the mouth.

The family's van was still in customs and as they had no car, Tom decided to take the bus to work. On the first day, as he exited the property gate and moved onto the street, he saw a man removing and replacing garbage can lids as he made his way down the block. A series of questions came as he watched this somewhat strange event. *Is this man looking for food? He seems too well dressed in his sports jacket and turtleneck. Could he be a terrorist?* Tom had heard about their activities. *What is he looking for and why is he opening garbage cans?*

As Tom strode out to the avenue and boarded a bus, these questions continued to swirl through his mind. Once on the bus, Tom walked down the aisle toward an empty seat. He could smell an obnoxious combination of tobacco and body odor. Quickly taking a seat, he tried to open a window but discovered that all the windows were sealed. At the next stop, an elderly woman, dressed completely in black and wearing a matching scarf on her head, boarded the bus. When she moved past, Tom could see she was carrying an umbrella and a shopping bag full of fresh market vegetables. As she was about to sit, a young male slipped in front of her. The elderly woman began to hit him on the arms and shoulders with her umbrella until he vacated the seat and went to stand in the front of the bus. That was the first and last time Tom rode the public bus.

After reaching the embassy, Tom reported the strange incident with garbage cans to the security person who immediately sent a team to investigate. The team reported that the "garbage can" man was the security chief for another embassy's ambassador whose residence was at the beginning of Tom's small, one-way street. Every morning, the foreign ambassador's security chief personally checked each garbage can for a potential bomb as his country as well as the United States were not well liked by the "Free Adria Movement." Only when satisfied would he allow the ambassador's car to proceed down the street and on to his embassy.

Why not take a Taxi?

Friends suggested that Tom take taxis instead of the bus and, for two weeks, he used this form of transportation.

Getting to work in the morning was not a major problem. The taxi drivers would stop and ask Tom where he wanted to go, and since he was going downtown, they would agree to take him. Usually, they had already stopped for other passengers and would pick up even more as they moved farther into the city. Though only two miles from work, Tom never knew when he would arrive, as it depended on how many other passengers there were and if their stop was before his. Hailing a cab in the evening was more problematic. The cab driver would ask Tom his destination, and if he didn't want to go there, he'd simply drive on. One evening, Tom read in the local Zarpathian Gazette that an old woman was left standing alone by the roadside one night in the mountains outside Zarpathia because the cab driver refused to take her any farther. When Tom had the opportunity to buy a used but functioning fire-engine-red Renault, he promptly purchased it and avoided taking the bus from that day forward.

"Don't worry, just be careful."

Once Tom began to drive to work, the embassy security guy asked him to stop by for a briefing. He explained, "You have only two ways to get to work from your home. If you look at a map, one route passes through small neighborhoods with narrow streets where you will encounter slow-moving traffic. There is a chance that there might be a 'Free Adria Movement' ambush or a car bomb awaiting you. The other route is straight down Mikhanoria Avenue to the front gate. If you take this option, you will be stuck in gridlocked traffic and a sitting duck. The 'Free Adria Movement' has used motorcycles with the passenger making the hit as the driver weaves through busy traffic."

His words were less than comforting.

The next morning, Tom had to wait in a line of vehicles at the gate while security guards checked under his car for a bomb. The security guy had told him to inspect under his car every morning, and it made no sense to have another check at the gate. Several years before, the "Free Adria Movement" had attacked the embassy by using a rocket shot from a nearby hillside. Being a sitting duck in a slow-moving queue beside the gate was not what Tom envisioned when he had accepted the Adria job. He thought, *A terrorist could simply approach the line of vehicles and shoot into the cars.*

Tom set out every morning trying to avoid the gridlock on the main avenue by cutting through the neighborhoods. Making his way along the narrow cobblestone streets while tensely holding the wheel, he tried to keep alert for suspicious parked vehicles, vans, and tailing motorcycles. Zarpathia, however, was full of motorcycles. Like ants swarming a piece of sugar, they were everywhere. He constantly heard the roar of their motors behind him. As he looked in the rearview mirror, his shoulders tensed, his fingers hurt from gripping the steering wheel, and adrenaline rushed through his body.

One day on his morning commute, he encountered a car parked in the middle of a narrow side street. He approached warily, saw no one in it, and decided to take a chance by driving up on the sidewalk to get around it. He damaged his car's steering column, and the vehicle limped to the embassy with a very wobbly, almost non-functional steering wheel.

Tom's wife Sheila had her own problems. Usually she and their American neighbor's wife walked their children to the bus stop so they could search for signs of potential danger. Tom thought, after hearing this, *If there is a terrorist incident, I don't know what our wives would have done except run. It would take much too long for the embassy to respond.* School bus stops and school buses, themselves, were soft targets. Sheila left for her U.S. Embassy job after the kids boarded the bus. As traffic worsened later in the day, she usually took over an hour to arrive. But there was one advantage. She left after the neighboring ambassador's security chief had checked all the trashcans for bombs.

Tom and Sheila's two boys attended the American School in a neighborhood on the other side of Zarpathia. They spent an hour each way on the school bus winding through avenues that were like parking lots and one-way side streets often blocked for construction. Sometimes the streets changed direction, making it impossible to determine in advance if they could be used or not. Almost every week, there was a bomb threat at the school. The kids returned home sunburnt from having waited for hours in the hot sun outside the school building while security checked for the non-existent bomb. Though it was always a prank, the school took the threats seriously.

Relax, play some tennis.

Playing tennis was one of the pastimes that took Tom's mind off the stressful life in Zarpathia. Tom's tennis buddy, Sal, lived in a nearby neighborhood atop a hill. While Tom's neighborhood was full of circles, small streets, and neatly manicured lawns and gardens, Sal and his wife lived in an isolated area where the homes were farther apart. The back windows of Sal's home overlooked the valley below where there were athletic fields and tennis courts. On sunny holidays, kids climbed to the top from the park below to catch the wind and fly their kites. Sal, with his erect military posture, thinning hair, and handlebar mustache, was a health nut and often walked the hilltop. He would stop to help the small kids having trouble getting their kites in the air. But what he most loved was tennis and trying to beat Tom, a player fifteen years his junior.

After dark, the athletic fields and tennis courts quickly emptied. With few streetlights and wild dogs roaming the area, it was not a place to be. These feral dogs, abandoned by owners who no longer wanted them or who just wanted to go on vacation without them, formed packs and roamed the area.

One warm summer evening, Sal and Tom were playing tennis on the courts below Sal's home. They were so focused on their fiercely competitive game, they hadn't noticed the fading light. Suddenly, the court lights went out and left them in utter darkness. The park's dim street lamps cast foreboding shadows as they hurriedly packed their things and began to climb back up the hill toward Sal's home. Halfway to the top, within view of the street lights above them, Sal pointed to some shadows moving rapidly in the dark below. "Dogs," he said. Grabbing their tennis racquets tightly, the two men prepared to fight for their lives but then decided to run instead. They crested the hill with the dogs yelping at their heels. The bright spotlights from Sal's house suddenly flashed on. They lit up the hill with artificial daylight and the dog pack, frightened by the glare, turned away. Sal's wife had unknowingly saved them. She offered them a stiff drink and, when she heard their story, told them she had assumed that it was so dark they would need light to find the back door.

Roll the Dice

In Zarpathia, safety was a matter of chance. One cold, wet November morning, the security guy announced that the previous evening, someone had rocket-attacked the German ambassador's apartment. A shoulder-launched rocket, shot from a car on the street below, had demolished the ambassador's third-floor street-front living room. Fortunately, the ambassador avoided death because he had just retired to his bedroom in the rear of the apartment.

Two days later, the police discovered the same car, with a bloodstained seat, parked near the port. Apparently, the perpetrator had wounded himself when he fired the rocket incorrectly. Although the anti-terrorist police could have gone to the army and checked military identity records, (military service was obligatory and blood type was on all records), they chose not to communicate with the military. The ambassador decided not to make a formal diplomatic complaint to the Adrian government, and the case was dropped.

At that moment, Tom thought, *We have passed through the looking glass in Lewis Carroll's* Alice *in* Wonderland. He had read the book as a youth and remembered that the Cheshire cat told Alice, "We're all mad here. I'm mad. You're mad." Zarpathia seemed to Tom to be just like the Mad Hatter's unanswerable riddle about what the raven and the writing desk had in common. (The answer is nothing.)

There was no apparent reason why the local government didn't challenge the terrorists, but street rumors speculated that it was because members of the current government had maintained certain relationships with radical groups in the past.

It seemed useless to turn to the police. One morning, all personnel were told they would have to vacate the Embassy by noon and return home. A representative of the police union had called and said there would be a police demonstration to protest low salaries. Tom and the rest of the staff went home as ordered and watched on TV as off-duty police officers threw Molotov cocktails at their compound's fence. There were no police to protect the buildings from the police, but the perimeter fence did its job and nothing burned down.

The Way We Treat Animals

Tom's mother saw the events on American TV and immediately called Tom and Sheila. She was concerned, but in the end, it did not quell her desire to visit Zarpathia. She arrived a few weeks later, and the family spent two weeks on a cruise on the East Adrian Sea. The trip was splendid until the Captain decided to return rapidly to Zarpathia so he could take on another tourist group. He removed the ship's stabilizers. The ship made excellent time but everyone on board got seasick and disembarked quickly when they reached port.

After returning to the mainland, Tom and Sheila took Mom to visit many of the local historic sites and temples along the coast. Only stones remained. This saddened Mom as she suddenly realized what little was left of the greatness that once was Adria.

Several days before Mom left, she and Tom were returning from a visit to see the grandkids in a play at the American School. As they drove through heavy traffic, a puppy appeared, trotting across a vehicular circle they had just entered. A tan mongrel with white paws and floppy ears, the dog, probably abandoned by its owner, was not aware of the danger until he felt the wind of cars rushing by. At that point, trembling and confused, he moved back and forth. Mom yelled, "Stop the car!"

Tom hit the brakes, not realizing she would open the door and try to jump out to save the puppy. As she began to step out, he quickly grabbed her arm and pulled her back inside. A few seconds later, a car hit the puppy. It moaned, yelped and then tried several times to stand before collapsing on the street as the car drove on and other cars simply avoided the now still body. "Mom, that could have been you," Tom said. The horns honked mercilessly behind and Tom was forced to drive on. Mom was silent for the rest of the trip home. Several days later, when Tom took her to the airport, she promised to visit Zarpathia again. She never did.

The Assassin School Bus

Each day when the kids returned from school, Tom and Sheila never knew what stories they would tell. There was the one about their French teacher who couldn't speak French, so she told the kids in English to speak French among themselves. Then there was their painful process of learning the local language. One year of study was obligatory at the school. They also recounted how they stood in the hot sun all day waiting for the all-clear sign after a bomb threat. Other stories involved school trips or visits to the beach. One day while at the beach, a rubber raft with kids on it was almost sucked out to sea by a rip tide because none of their teachers could swim. The most striking story was the one about the "assassin school bus."

Near the end of the family's stay in Zarpathia, the kids were on the bus traveling from their school toward home. The older son had the window seat while the younger sat on the inside. According to the older son, an old woman, not noticing the bus, began to cross the street. She then disappeared from view. The bus stopped and as Tom's son looked out the window, he saw the woman lying on the ground with people surrounding her. The bus driver opened the door and jumped out. Apparently, the bus had struck the woman and knocked her down. Some police officers arrived and, while they interrogated the driver, the bus full of kids remained stationary for about an hour. When the driver reentered the bus, the woman was still lying on the ground. He began screaming in broken English, "It is all your fault. You kids always make the trouble. You kill this old woman."

Tom's two boys, who had been sitting quietly talking, were flabbergasted. The younger boy had seen nothing so he only knew what the driver told them. The older boy, traumatized, believed the bus had killed the woman. For the next few days, he called the bus the "assassin bus." In truth, Tom later learned that the bus had not killed the woman. She had died from a heart attack caused by being knocked down by the bus. *Either way,* Tom thought, *my kids are not responsible for the driver's ineptness and extremely aggressive driving.* It was just like the Adrians to shift the blame, whether it was the death of an old woman or territorial issues with their neighbors. Surprisingly, the Adrians did not blame the United States for crimes such as theft, rape, or murder, only for economic exploitation. According to the inhabitants of Zarpathia, the gypsies or immigrants committed all these local crimes. It was never an Adrian.

Time to Leave

One day, when Tom was more philosophic, he mused, *Death dealing takes many forms. Terrorists use assassinations, bombings, and rocket attacks. Some Adrians of good will have promised to help, but somehow, nothing is ever done. When people forget the value of life, any life, they are committing moral suicide. In Zarpathia, everyone proudly tells you about the city's "Golden Time" when their culture left the world a heritage of reason, order, and humanity.* But then Tom remembered what Gandhi said, "The greatness of a nation can be judged by the way animals are treated."

After two years, Tom, Sheila, and their kids left Zarpathia for Tom's next assignment. All of them welcomed the opportunity to drive, walk, go to school, and take a cab or bus without being a target or observing more death. A few months after they left, a newspaper article appeared in the *International Herald Tribune* referring to the recent death of a foreign Defense attaché in Zarpathia. The group "Free Adria Movement" shot him dead while he was driving to work on Mikhanoria Avenue.

18
RAIN AND FIRE

"I mean, you know, we don't live in a perfect world."
Michael Bloomberg

TOM WAS WATCHING A SOAP opera in the upstairs TV room when his wife Sheila yelled, "What's that noise? Don't you hear it? It sounds like a helicopter." When he ran to the back window, Tom saw a small helicopter circling the luxurious mansion adjacent to their older home. Tom moved to the front window just as the sound of shots rang out from the street below.

"Get away from the window," Sheila yelled. "You know we've seen TV reports showing how the police killed more innocent bystanders than criminals during their shoot-outs." Sheila was right. Tom remembered hostages on a bus, kids playing in the streets, people outside banks, all victims of the Tuparian police's inability to shoot straight.

Although the couple lived in Cerradina, the capital, the rules of engagement still applied and so did the collateral damage.

Two police cars were parked outside their house in the cul-de-sac. The officers took cover behind their cars while firing at someone in the neighbor's home. A SWAT van pulled up and police with shotguns jumped out and began firing as well.

Tom picked up the phone and called the embassy. "Security, we've got a world war going on outside my home," he said.

"We'll send someone right over," they replied.

Within fifteen minutes, an embassy security car pulled in and parked next to the two police cars and the SWAT van. Shortly, two men knocked at their door. One was short and dark complexioned and the other, taller and lighter in skin color. "We're from the embassy," the taller one said.

"Good," Tom replied. "What's going on?"

"Stay inside the house," he said. "Don't go out. Two bandidos are in the next house and the famíla is being held hostage." The family's older son had escaped out the window and notified the police that his home had been invaded. The two security men told Tom the third bandido went out the back just as the police opened fire. The helicopter chased him across the field behind the home. From inside the home, the two others returned fire and refused to give up. Apparently, the family ran a jewelry business and kept many of their items in a safe at home. That's what the criminals were after. The embassy security men checked with the police and then brought Tom up to date. "The bandidos are still returning fire but know they are outgunned and will probably be shot if they don't give up."

An hour later, hearing no more shots, the police stormed the house, broke down the door, and entered, only to find the bandits had fled. The father, mother, and two younger children were alone, tied to chairs at the dining room table. The home invaders had disappeared into the night. The embassy security men left, the SWAT van left, and one of the police cars drove off. The second police car remained; for their security, they were told. The helicopter circled the area long into the night. Everything returned to normal, whatever normal was in Cerradina.

The Dystopian City

The first time Tom was posted to Cerradina, he learned that when they built the city, the government hired a communist architect whose urban plan divided the capitol into various residential, commercial, and government sectors. The center of the city contained government office buildings and ministries. Every weekend, government officials, elected politicians, and businessmen caught a Friday night flight home to their home towns and only returned Sunday night or Monday morning. Cerradina was geographically in the middle of the country and in the middle of nowhere. If a nuclear war broke out, it would be the safest place in the world.

George Orwell's vision of a cookie cutter society became reality for Tom. On this flat, high plain where the vastness of the domed sky and the flatness of the terrain would have dwarfed any other type of architecture, the buildings needed to be larger than life. The whole city resembled a Soviet monolith from the Cold War, an Orwellian dystopia, a futuristic dream full of possibilities that would always remain unfulfilled.

The streets and buildings were numbered. Sectors were designated by functional names such as commercial, hotel, bank, residential, club, and embassy sectors. In the residential areas, five-story brick apartment buildings, like somber mausoleums, clustered in neighborhoods that were organized into smaller units. Each apartment had a block number, a building number, and an apartment number.

Embassy functionaries with families lived on the opposite side of an artificial lake in houses with gardens and pools. One of two bridges had to be crossed to get there. Like ants at the beginning and end of the day, a multitude of black and white vehicles crossed the lake on these bridges. The Lake Area with its large homes and verdant compounds stood in juxtaposition to the city's spider web of elevated avenues accessed by a dizzying array of on/off ramps rising in a circular pattern from the streets below.

In the city, the shopping areas resembled small rural towns or Wild West cities with stores stacked up against each other along dusty streets with diagonal front-end parking. The commercial areas consisted of small shops collocated by what they sold. Groceries and drinks had their own street, car repair another, electronics another, and tools another.

This functionality was the antithesis of the Tuparian affinity for a crazy mix of color, chaos, and charm. After Tom arrived, he often wondered if this was the creators' attempt to come to terms with the country's schizophrenic mixture of warmth and violence. The architects of Cerradina endeavored to build an egalitarian, colorless, classless society where everyone was the same. But everyone was not the same. The downtown apartments differed from the large houses with pools across the lake. Multitudes of poor people were housed outside the capital in smaller cities. These poorer workers rode to their jobs on a light rail system that closed down at eight p.m. to prevent criminals from accessing the capital at night. The creators built the city in defiance of human and physical nature.

Can you Change Human Nature?

The city's inability to control its crime was abundantly clear. During his first assignment in Cerradina, the capital of Tuparia, and before getting his downtown apartment, Tom temporarily resided in the hotel area. It was located near the only major shopping center and the bus station. It should have been safe at night but he could not even cross the area on foot and had to take a taxi. The builders did not make sidewalks for pedestrians.

The nightclub across the street from Tom's hotel was a great place to listen to jazz, but he had to let the poorly educated, scantily clad "companions" practice their minimal English with him and had to buy them a drink. These girls would always ask the customers, "O senhor quer companhia?" If you answered "*Sim,*" they would take you upstairs to a private room. Whether at the bar or upstairs, it was necessary to ask for a chilled drink in the original bottle, unopened with no ice added. Tom knew if the bottle was open, he could never be sure what substance might have been added to his drink.

Crime was not limited to the pickpockets who lurked and robbers who assaulted pedestrians. The first time Tom attended language class at the American Cultural Center, he parked his rented VW bug in front of the building. When he returned after class, it was gone. Running to the Center's door, he asked the guard in a panicked voice, "Have you seen my VW bug?" The guard was immensely sympathetic and replied, "Sinto muito senhor, mais eu não vi nada." (He didn't see anything.) There were only two ways in and out of Cerradina, north or south, and the police watched both. Later, Tom learned that the police were involved in the trade of stolen vehicles which were resold across the border in a neighboring country.

The poor marginalized class produced many of the country's criminals, but Tom soon found they did not have a monopoly on crime. When he thought about it, Tom realized the capital's ultramodern buildings, judicial offices, congress, and towering modernistic glass cathedral made it look civilized, but the founders' proclivity for futuristic structures did not eliminate greed and corruption. Modernity could not suppress the orgy-like spending that afflicted the "new rich" who spent millions on drugs, cars, and designer clothes. The criminals in the beach cities who preyed on tourists were really no different from the hypocritical political class, the hedonistic socialites, or the corrupt businessmen.

Rain and Fire

The capital's creators with their dreams of modernity

not only failed to create a new society, they failed in their attempt to defy nature. When Tom wanted to take up sailing at the local Yacht Club, he was told a bacterium in the lake would eat his liver if he stepped in the water or fell off a boat. It could be fatal. But this did not stop Tom. On courageous afternoons, while sailing on the artificial lake and avoiding falling overboard, he gazed at the cotton-like clouds that embraced and then released the blazing sun. The aqua water mirrored their near perfect construction. The sky seemed to go on forever. The nearby waterfalls spewed dazzling drops of water that fell like liquid sunlight onto the rocks below.

Water was a magical elixir, a touch of life itself, and a few magical drops could turn the dusty barren high plain into a wonderland of red, yellow, white, and purple hibiscus, flowering cactus, avocados, and palm trees. But the rain could also be dangerous. During the wet season's monsoon storms, there were times when the airport diverted incoming planes to the nearest city because they could not land in the downpour. One afternoon, while driving along one of the main axis roads, Tom was caught in one of these intense thunderstorms. The road quickly flooded and his car aquaplaned across four lanes of traffic before he was able to regain control. Fortunately, it was one of the bigger avenues, and although the car slid through three inches of rain on a smooth cement surface, it safely came to rest after hitting the curb several times.

Rain was not the only hazard. There was also fire. One day during the dry season, Tom drove outside the capital into the dusty countryside. Suddenly the road ahead filled with smoke. He saw little flashes of red eating the dry vegetation bordering one side of the road. As the flames jumped to the other side, the way forward became impassable. The scene resembled a California-style brush fire, and it grew in size before his eyes. He averted disaster by reversing and choosing another route back to the city. The fire followed in pursuit and for the next few days, the winds and dry conditions made breathing difficult.

Rita, a Hope for the Future

After a few months, Tom hired a housemaid named Rita. She came from one of the city slums that surrounded the capital and, as a direct descendent of the manual workers who built the city, she was part of the first generation born there. Rita was in her late twenties and had a daughter when she was just eighteen. She was raising the child as a single mother and wanted her daughter to have a better life. She made sure the little girl went to school and paid relatives to take care of the girl during the day. To get to Tom's apartment she took several buses, and her days were long and hard.

Rita was pretty in a Zoe Saldana way. She was thinner and looked older than the popular Dominican-American actress. Her hair was pulled back severely in a bun, and she wore large, oval glasses through which her big brown eyes surveyed the world. Unlike Lourdes, a heavy-set jovial woman who cooked for Tom's neighbors and hailed from the northeast, Rita was serious in a melancholy way. She was a quick learner and figured out what Tom liked to eat and how to take care of the apartment. She paid attention to things like the extra propane tanks that were stored on the back stairway and made sure they were not leaking. Rita knew very well that if the building's elevators stopped, the back stairs descending past the propane tanks were the only way out. Lourdes, less detail-oriented than Rita, was badly burned in a propane fire caused by a faulty canister.

One morning, Rita asked if she could buy cauliflower and a chicken that she wanted to cook for dinner. She brought home a wonderful white head of the vegetable, but when she dropped the cauliflower into water mixed with bleach, menacing looking white worms appeared from behind the leaves. Rita's chicken almost killed Tom due to the amount of salt it contained. "O senhor não gosta?" she said, looking at Tom with both judgment and sorrow. Tom knew it was inedible but choked some down not to hurt her feelings.

"It's only got a bit too much salt," he gasped. "Next time, if you could not use salt that would be good." Rita wanted to succeed, and Tom thought he had resolved the issue, but the next chicken was just as salty. Puzzled, Tom asked her, "Rita, você usou sal?" She swore that she had not used salt, but he later discovered Rita did not believe garlic salt was salt.

When Sheila, Tom's fiancée, a blonde cowgirl from the state of Rio Grande do Sul, Brazil, came to visit, Tom could tell that Rita was uncomfortable. They were a study in contrasts, the dark skinned, dark haired native of Tuparia and the blue-eyed, blonde-haired farm girl from the Brazilian south. Rita was used to having Tom to herself, making food and cleaning his clothes. She felt threatened by another female presence. She squinted through her glasses at Sheila, her cheeks crinkled, and her overall expression resembled a dark rainstorm rolling in on a sunny day.

Sheila didn't visit Cerradina often before they were married, so Rita continued as always until Tom left Tuparia, married Sheila, and then took an assignment at another overseas post. Tom would always remember Rita who, like Cerradina, was young and hopeful. She and this strange dream city were growing up together. Tom never found out what became of Rita, but he did return to Cerradina.

Return to Cerradina

Many years later, when Tom and Sheila returned to Cerradina, they were accompanied by their two young boys and lived across the lake in a very different part of town. The city had changed, grown larger, and downtown was more congested. Living across the lake among the rich Cerradinians was quite different from the downtown bachelor quarters where Tom had lived during his first assignment there.

One of their neighbors, a local judge, built a soccer field on his property and kept the huge annoying floodlights turned on all night, making sleep difficult. It was all about letting his sons and their friends practice when they wanted. On weekends, he threw huge noisy parties that ended at five in the morning. Later, one of his sons was accused of raping a girl during one of these parties. Somehow the girl disappeared, and there was no one to testify against his son.

As their home was quite large, the couple soon hired a day maid named Josie. Unlike Rita, Josie spent her time on the phone with her friends discussing the problems she had with her unfaithful husband and with her small child whom she really didn't like. After the couple fired Josie, they went through a series of house cleaners, some more honest than others but never found one that resembled Rita in her willingness to work hard and improve herself.

Big John, a Light in the Darkness

During this stay in Cerradina, the family took a four-day vacation to a beach town known for its spectacular views. When still single, Tom had visited the city and his towel, jacket, sandals, and small cash wallet were stolen while he waded in the water. This time, with his family along, Tom decided to take more precautions and hired a motorista to drive them around the city. The agency he called sent them a tall, burley black fellow named "Big John."

"Big John" had spent some time in the police, had formerly been a driver for a foreign consulate, and now worked for a Scottish/British tourism group. When he first met Tom and Sheila, he told them about an Israeli couple, his previous clients. Apparently, the couple was walking near the beach when they were robbed. Big John, seeing what had transpired, stuck out his foot and tripped the thief as he ran by. John grabbed him with his meaty sledgehammer hands and hit the thief in the face. Then he reached into the criminal's pocket, pulled out the Israeli tourist's wallet, which was full of cash, and returned it to the stunned couple. They hired him on the spot to be their bodyguard for the length of their stay at the beach city.

John took Tom and his family everywhere, including scenic overlooks, magnificent monuments, the colonial sector, the slums, museums, and all the beaches. He was armed with a Glock 17, but his physical presence was enough to scare off thieves and general pickpockets. One night, John was driving them to a restaurant when he turned down a narrow side street. He began tapping the wheel with a nervous rhythm. "Voce vê este vehiculo estacionado ali?" Tom saw the car he mentioned, parked in a suspicious manner outside a small convenience store. Two men were inside and the car lights were off. "Eles vão assaltar o dono quando ele sair," he whispered. (They will rob the store or the owner when he comes out.)

A man, who appeared to be the owner, exited with keys in hand, locked the door, and began pulling a metal gate across the front. At the same time, the two men jumped out of the car and began moving quickly toward him. The owner, seeing the two approaching, took out a pistol and pointed it at the men. As both sides began to fire, Big John wisely hit the gas and left without waiting to see who was left standing. John kept his word and kept the family safe until they left the beach town and returned to the capitol.

The Jewelry People

The neighbors who shared the family's cul-de-sac were standoffish, did not talk to them, and appeared not to care about anyone. One day, the neighbor's car, driven by the wife's chauffeur, hit Sheila's vehicle as the chauffeur was exiting their small cul-de-sac. The wife, who was in the car at the time of the accident, told Sheila, "My chauffeur will pay, it's his responsibility." Later, she agreed that since her chauffeur had no insurance, she would pay. In spite of her diamonds and chic clothing, she never did and Sheila had to pay for the damage. Sheila and Tom knew little about them so they were surprised when the neighbors were the victims of a home invasion.

Tom often wondered how the wife fared during the robbery and the following firefight between criminals and police. After it was over, the couple refused to testify against the robbers because the attackers had threatened to kill their family. The details of the home invasion were never published, but Tom often imagined in detail the events that took place that day.

He pictured the wife's reaction when the three intruders entered her home. She would have been dismissive, bullying, and superior. That is until they put the gun to her head and threatened to cut off her daughter's finger unless she gave them the jewelry safe combination. She would have been protective of her spoiled kids and would have called to her older son upstairs. He would not have heard her over the loud metal rock he played on his CD player. She would have told her husband to do something, and he would have remained silent while they tied and gagged him. When he saw them put the gun to his wife's head, he would have given up his cell phone, wallet, diamond ring, and silver cufflinks without resistance. The younger children would have cried until the gags stifled the noise. They would have sat facing each other, tied to the dining room chairs and praying that they would remain alive. The parents wouldn't have known that the older son had come downstairs to get a cold beer, seen what was going on, escaped out of an upper-story window, and run to the police. The police loud speaker and the gunfight that broke out with bullets piercing glass and wood and flying in every direction would have terrified them.

The day after the home invasion, a police car parked in the couple's cul-de-sac. It remained there for two weeks and then disappeared. The "jewelry people" also disappeared and there was a for sale sign in front of their home. Perhaps they had gone somewhere with more walls, stronger gates, better alarms, somewhere where the darkness could not reach them. But Tom knew they could never get away from their own inner darkness.

Tom and Sheila left the city shortly after and returned to the United States. Back in the states, Tom reflected on his stay in Cerradina. He remembered the majesty of clouds in an endless blue sky overlooking waterfalls and flowers but also the dangers wrought by the elements of fire and rain. He considered Cerradina to be a naïve attempt at social engineering based on the futile desire to abolish crime and poverty. For him, it was the result of a misguided faith in a future that would never happen. But he also remembered the warmth and courage of a people brought low by greed and violence. Memories of the criminals and the "jewelry people" fought in his mind with those of Big John and Rita. Tom wanted to believe that light would overcome darkness. In the end he decided that he, like Cerradina's founders, was at heart a naïve idealist.

19

THE LAST MAN AT THE TABLE

TIM LOOKED UP AS SEÑOR Carreca glided toward the table and slipped into an empty seat. The older man wore a cream-colored double-breasted suit over a pale blue dress shirt that matched his eyes. His gold tie had a Mallard duck pattern. The bottle green and brown ducks with black rear ends and orange bills reminded Tim of a pond near his parent's home in North Carolina. The Mallards wintered there. Carreca had carefully selected the tie as part of his approach. Later, Tim learned that the older man, a clinical psychiatrist as well as diplomat, never did anything without a reason.

Carreca, fifteen years Tim's elder, was fifty-five. With receding gray hair and a bald spot on top, Carreca's leather-like tanned skin made him look much older. His hawkish nose and beady eyes reminded Tim of a bird of prey. When Tim first met him on a diplomatic tour bus during a visit to a vineyard outside the capitol of Calimbria, Carreca had seemed friendly.

Tim had been in Calimbria for a year. He was now familiar with the Spanish-speaking nation whose European ancestors had come with the conquistadors and intermarried with the local Indian populace. Carreca had arrived in Huatucla, the country's capitol, two years before Tim. The well-dressed older man was a First Secretary at the embassy of a Marxist country whose relations with the U.S. had chilled.

During the wine tasting, Tim ended up seated next to Señor Carreca. While they tasted the fruity red medium-bodied Pinot noirs infused with blackberries, cherries, and plums, and the light-bodied dryer and pungent white Sauvignon Blancs with a hint of citrus, Tim introduced himself. Carreca responded by offering his name and his position at his embassy. Tim had studied Marxism in Europe, and he easily kept up with his new acquaintance during their impassioned discussion of Marx, Engels, and the application of Marxist theory to Latin America. Carreca seemed outwardly enamored with this "strange" young gringo who had multiple postings in Latin America and expressed his opinions in fluent Spanish.

After the wine tasting ended, the two remained together during a visit to a bird sanctuary near the vineyard. Tim mentioned that his parent's home overlooked a preserve for birds and waterfowl. Carreca seemed fascinated and especially interested when Tim mentioned how much he enjoyed the Mallards. The older man was passionate about the gray heron and said the bird was both native to his country and to the wetlands of the eastern U.S.

On the trip back to Huatulca, Carreca suggested that they get together for lunch and plan a day of bird watching. Tim politely accepted. This Marxist diplomat, who would meet one-on-one with an American despite his country's non-fraternization policy with U.S. persons, intrigued him. Carreca, with his warm, friendly, relaxed demeanor, seemed different from his compatriots. There was none of the usual anti-U.S. rhetoric.

The lunch never took place. Tim was called away when his father-in-law suffered a stroke. When he returned, Tim discovered that Carreca was on vacation. Tim surmised that he was probably back home, although when he called, the embassy never confirmed this. Several months later, Carreca called to reschedule the lunch. He suggested breakfast instead at a conveniently located hotel in downtown Huatulca called the "El Nuevo Presidente". The hotel was an old brick building painted a rose color and looked a bit like the Argentine president's "Casa Rosa" in Buenos Aires. As it was only a few blocks from his home, Tim walked there.

Tim arrived first and took a seat upstairs in the breakfast area. Carreca, who had taken a taxi from his embassy, showed up a bit later sporting a smile and confident air. He apologized for being late but mentioned the traffic. In the narrow cobblestone streets of downtown historic Huatucla, traffic tended to bottleneck at every stop light. On the wider avenues, Calimbrians usually made left-hand turns from the far right and moved across up to three lanes of traffic to make their turn. Foreign drivers had to move more slowly to avoid an accident. The taxi drivers just drove like lunatics.

"Ola Tim. Como andas?" Carreca began in a friendly tone.

"Nice tie, Señor Carreca," Tim replied. "Is it Italian or from your country?"

"Italia," Carreca replied. "But they make just as good ties en mi pais and the ducks are just as beautiful."

The second-floor breakfast café was decorated with brown wicker chairs and glass tabletops. The tables were placed around an open shaft surrounded by a glass enclosure. The open area ran up all five floors of the hotel, allowing sunlight to shine in from above. At nine-thirty in the morning, the café was almost vacant. Most of the guests had finished breakfast and proceeded to their day's activities.

Calimbria attracted tourists from other Latin countries and executives from the U.S. It had a large U.S. interest section at the embassy, which dealt with U.S. citizens who lived, worked, or visited Calimbria.

Carreca had left his suit jacket unbuttoned. As he sat down, he appeared to focus intently on Tim, and unconsciously ran his left hand over his jacket to brush out the wrinkles. Strangely, he did not order breakfast. After the waiter had brought glasses of water, Carreca dismissed him with a wave of the hand saying, "Pedimos mas tarde." He then turned to Tim.

As Carreca leaned forward, the ever-present smile remained frozen on his face. He began to speak in a rapid but hushed Spanish, "Señor Tim, you told me at the wine tasting that the U.S. and my country should have better relations. We need someone like you to help us make this happen. If you truly want our peoples to live in peace and prosperity, you must help us. If we knew what your country wanted from us and what it planned to do as regards our country, we could do much to improve relations." Carreca kept talking, not allowing Tim to insert a word until he had finished speaking.

Carreca's words surprised Tim, and he stared down at his water glass trying to avoid any immediate answer. He needed time to think. Why would Carreca think that he would provide him such information? They were not friends and had spent almost no time together.

When he looked up, Tim's brown eyes met Carreca's light blue eyes. There was something different about the man. His eyes had turned darker and steelier. Clearly, there was a lot more to the man than Tim had imagined.

Tim lips quivered slightly, and he took a deep breath before making his counter proposal. "Señor Carreca," he said, "we both agree that relations between our countries need to improve, but I see things a bit differently than you do. Simply withdrawing our economic sanctions will not help. Your government has ruined your economy and cost your people their freedom. I need you to stand up and help your people. Only a person like you can make a difference. Please help me to help your country."

Carreca's habitual smile disappeared. His eyes grew larger and his eyebrows arched. "Señor Tim, what are you saying to me?" he hissed.

Tim replied with a smile. "I'm asking you to do what you wanted me to do."

"Dios, what do you think I was asking you to do?" Carreca said, his voice now shrill and cold.

"Now that we understand each other," Tim said, "let's

order some breakfast like two normal people."

Carreca pushed away from the table and abruptly stood up, almost overturning his chair. "I can never be friends with you, Señor Tim," he said as he threw his napkin on the table. "You are not a friend of me or my country." He turned like a marionette and marched off without looking back.

Later, when he reviewed the encounter in his mind, Tim figured it must have been his training, "always be prepared, expect the unexpected." But he found, despite the deodorant he was wearing, that his shirt had wet circles under his armpits. He remained seated and calmed his nerves.

For a brief moment, he thought, *I'll have an espresso and one of the hotel's renowned homemade buttered croissants.* He had done well. Nevertheless, he knew he immediately had to tell his boss what had happened.

Tim returned to the office to report the incident. Carreca had thrown him a curve, but he survived. His boss might puzzle over it and wonder what had brought on this approach, but Tim knew he would eventually pat him on the back. Tim smiled. He had held his own and perhaps even won. He was the last man at the table.

Turn the page for an exciting preview of Christian Pascale's next book, *Windows of Heaven*.

TOM ZIPPED HIS SKI JACKET closed to protect himself against the cold. In 2050, mid-September now resembled late December. He wore jeans, a three-colored flannel shirt, and a clashing woolen scarf he found in an abandoned dorm room. A worn blue ski hat covered his unruly brown hair. His battery-operated electric razor had disappeared, and he had been unable to locate a regular safety razor. His several weeks of beard growth showed a mixture of brown and reddish stubble. He had never been able to grow a mustache; the area over his mouth looked like he had wiped a dirty hand over his upper lip.

As he stood on the bluffs overlooking College Avenue, Tom's piercing blue eyes surveilled the town of Easton. After *Surge Saturday,* the former Delaware River had become a bay stretching to the east and covering the area where Philadelphia once stood. With nightfall approaching, Tom hoped his sister, Helene, would return quickly. She would return by climbing College Avenue and soon it would be too dark to see her.

Tom reached for the candy bar he had slipped into the front pocket of his pants. He had rummaged through his car for half an hour and found only the one candy bar. The car sat useless as it was a hybrid gas/solar/electric vehicle and there were no functioning charging stations, little sun and no gas being pumped in the Easton area.

Digging into his jeans, he felt the tightness caused by the paperback New Testament he had placed in his back pocket. His mother had given him the book several years ago, and he wondered how long it would be before its prophetic visions came true. Pulling it out in the failing light, he reread some underlined words from the Gospel of Luke: *And there shall be signs in the sun, and in the moon, and in the stars; and upon the earth distress of nations, with perplexity; the sea and the waves roaring. Men's hearts failing them for fear… The sun shall be turned into darkness, and the moon into blood… (Luke 25#21)*

The earth's ice caps had substantially melted, the waves of the sea had roared, volcanoes had spewed fire, nations had been in great distress, a meteorite had struck the earth, and men's hearts had failed for fear. What else could happen?

***

Tom was worried about his sister. When he arrived on the Friday before the fateful day the world changed, she had asked about their mom and dad. Tom said he had called that morning and they were fine. The next morning, as they packed the car to get an early start, the news was broadcast on the car radio that Washington, D.C. no longer existed. "They're okay. They made it out. They'll call us," she said.

Looking at her with all the tenderness he could muster, Tom said, "Maybe you're right, but it took out the greater D.C. area. It's now ocean. Still, we could hear from them." Then there was no electricity, no satellites or cell phones, and the world fell silent except for long-range radio. Helene refused to accept what Tom knew to be fact.

Their parents now missing if not dead, Tom wanted to take Helene back to Blacksburg. The original volcanic activity and then the ice and snow caused by the oncoming new Ice Age had made travel over the last weeks too dangerous. So they stayed put in Easton, trying to wait out the weather. Lafayette College closed and over the following three weeks, it had become the home of a lost orphaned group of former students and refugees living in their snowy citadel, separate from the city below. The inhabitants survived by using what food remained in the college cafeteria freezers, but un-replenished food supplies were now running low.

About a week after *Surge Saturday* came the shocking news that the new Capital of the United States along with its weak transitional government, now in Albuquerque, New Mexico, had fallen to the paramilitary soldiers of the Black Sun.

ABOUT THE AUTHOR

Christian Pascale was born in Brooklyn, New York. He graduated from Lafayette College Magna Cum Lauda with degrees in French and International Relations. At Lafayette, he was inducted into the Phi Beta Kappa honor society and then went on to receive an M.A. in European Area Studies from American University in Washington D.C. and a Doctorat de l'université from La Sorbonne in Paris, France. During his early years, he worked as a substitute teacher, a tennis instructor in Europe and the U.S., a teacher of English as a Foreign Language, a political fundraiser, and Director of Studies at a New England preparatory school. For more than thirty years, he worked in both domestic and foreign assignments for the United States Government.

Christian is also a poet who has published fifteen poems in two internationally distributed magazines and is currently a member of the James City Poets. He is married to Liria Hoffmann Pascale who is a native Brazilian and an architect. They live in Williamsburg, Virginia and have two adult sons.